James Spence

James is a dreamer with far too much time on his hands. He lives with his wife Tiff, and cat Angel, in Dunfermline, Scotland where he dreams, schemes and screams in delight when he receives yet another brand new T-shirt through the post.

He is the creator of *Dr Sheep and the Aardvark*, unquestionably one of Scotland's most popular on-line comic strips, enjoyed by thousands of comic fans around the world.

One of his poems was recently published by Google in their book *Search Me* by Neil Taylor. They also sent him 2 T-shirts!

Silly Beggar

The World's Stupidest Begging Letters

James Spence

AURORA METRO PRESS

This volume first published in Great Britain 2009 by Aurora Metro Publications Ltd, 67 Grove Avenue, Twickenham, TW1 4HX www.aurorametro.com

With thanks to: Aidan Jenkins, Neil Gregory, Gabriele Maurer, Simon Bennett, Carmel Walsh, Cordelia Makartsev, Phil Gibbs and all the companies who got into the spirit of this book.

Editing and production: Cheryl Robson

Photographs and layout: Tiffany Spence © 2009 Tiffany Spence

Cover, illustrations and graphics: James Spence © 2009 James Spence

Printed by Ashford Colour Press, Fareham, Hants UK .

ISBN 978 -1- 906582-03-6

For my wife Tiffany, my cat Angel

and my good friend and house guest Dr Sebastian

Let's start at the beginning...

Having graduated, married and bought a house within a matter of months of each other, my bank account was well and truly annihilated. With a mortgage relentlessly soaking up cash, more bills than a duck after a cloning accident and nothing in the entertainment budget, things looked decidedly bleak. Cash-wise, I was just breaking even - and this was long before anyone had heard of the Credit Crunch. But I wasn't about to let it get me down. With time on my hands, and an Internet connection, I decided to do something about it - and have some fun in the process!

The book you hold in your hands right now contains the weird and wacky emails I sent to high street stores, manufacturers and multi-national companies (even to my favourite breakfast take-away) designed to encourage them to share their promotional goodies with one of their valued customers, that being me!

Throughout these pages you are invited to join in the fun as the Customer Services departments of large corporations are fed ridiculous stories enticing them to part with their sweet logo-bearing bounty.

To begin with, I sent my targets short poems. Almost immediately, parcels started arriving at my door. Encouraged by this I changed tactics and gave my emails a letter format. My victims immediately latched on to the spirit of the game. As I made the letters more outlandish, filling them with hare-brained tales, jokes and the antics of Angel, our cat, the goodies continued to arrive.

It wasn't long before I discovered that the sillier the content, the better the freebies! Perhaps this was the result of my begging missives helping to lighten the working days of overworked Customer Service Executives as they toiled through in-trays piled high with routine, boring correspondence. And there's certainly nothing remotely routine about tales of heroic alter-egos, strange cloning experiments, penguin attacks, the production of forest smells and many more weird and wonderful fables, each crafted to acquire goodies completely free of charge.

Until I began this project, I had thought of giant companies as faceless entities, but now my perception of the corporate world has changed forever. Companies are people too!

If there's one thing I learned in the making of this book it's that if you don't ask, you don't get; and its all about how you ask. If you want something for nothing, you have to make maximum use of your ingenuity gene and be prepared to do some serious buttering-up!

In the midst of our global economic crisis where money is tight all round, *Silly Beggar* offers a fun way of getting your hands on great items.

I would like to thank all those who entered into the spirit of this project for replying, sending awesome loot and, most of all, for being great sports.

Group hug!

James Spence

To: Blockbuster Video
From: James Spence
Subject: Mental Rental

Hi there Blockbusters,

I have a sorry story to tell. It is a story of a man, his love of DVDs and pizza...

I am a member of the Blockbuster DVD Rental Club. It has been a pleasure being a member so far and I really feel like 'part of the gang'. I have always received my DVDs promptly, in good condition and without the need for sadness or regret. This was also the case the other day when I ordered and received the DVD 'Jam', a comedy show from your fine organisation.

I ordered a pizza (my favourite pepperoni and prune) and fried up an egg for putting atop the pizza (my local pizza place does not make a fried egg pizza... yet). I changed into my favourite DVD-watching tee shirt (it has an owl on it) whilst watching said 'Jam' DVD.

The show promptly began and I found myself at first tittering, then laughing, then guffawing at the various sketches and gags. Before I knew it, I was hooting like the very owl on my shirt!! But humour turned to tears as disaster struck midway through episode 4...

During the episode, so engrossed was I in the show, that I failed to notice the fragile nature of the pizza slice in my hand until it was too late. I heard a subtle but all-too-memorable phump!-

You guessed it, DVD-buddies, the pizza landed on my owl tee. It was covered in margarita sauce, pepperoni, prune, fried egg and some chilli sauce I had added to 'pep it up a bit'.

I have since tried and tried to wash the offending marks out, but they've left a permanent stain. What on Earth is in that chilli sauce? Tattoos?!!

Yes, I know that Blockbusters is not even remotely responsible for this. It's clearly my local pizza makers' fault! However, after several lengthy conversations with them, it turns out they can't offer me any replacement tee shirts. They didn't even offer to refund the money I paid for the pizza, egg and sauce!! Outrageous!

Anyway, I wanted to contact you to ask if you happened to have a spare (large) Blockbuster tee shirt that I could wear whilst watching your fine DVDs in future. I won't spill pizza on it!!

Can't wait to hear from you.

Thanks for all your fantastic work,

James Spence

To: James Spence
From: Blockbuster Video
Subject: Re: Mental Rental

Dear James,

Thank you for your e-mail.

We sympathise greatly with your present dilemma. Nobody understands the bond between a man and his TV T-Shirt quite like us here at Blockbuster where it seems to be law that you must be a chronic movie buff! Many of us here have also fallen foul of the dreaded falling pizza, ruining your precious TV T-Shirt that holds so many memories, with whom you've been through so much!

However we here are fortunate enough to have an abundance of readily available T-Shirts to help ease situations like these. We understand that not everyone can have such luxuries and so have happily sent you a brand new TV T-Shirt with a charming Kill Bill logo on it, we chose this one as it is red and yellow so if you do happen to drop any pizza onto it, it shouldn't show too much!

There are also a few complimentary extras in the post too. We have sent you an American Pie 3 poster and a rather fetching pair of Shrek ears which we hope you will wear like a crown proudly, and spare a little thought for us here at Customer Services every time you adorn them.

Kind Regards and Happy Viewing,

Richard Smith

Blockbuster Online Team

TEE SHIRT, SHREK EARS AND AMERICAN PIE MOVIE POSTER

To: Xerox
From: James Spence
Subject: Duped

Hi there,

I write to let you know about something that happened to me the other day at work.

My story begins several days ago. I sat at my desk and realised that no one had phoned or emailed in days. In addition to this, none of my work colleagues had disturbed me in a long time either. I was thoroughly bored and started wondering if my life was being taken from me for the sake of the big man!

I glanced to my right and spotted the office Xerox copier. This started me thinking of an ingenious idea. If the only thing that was keeping the pay cheques coming was my physical presence, then if I could make a copy of myself, I could leave it propped up in my chair. I might just get away with it.

I immediately started pressing parts of my body against the Xerox machine, duplicating my features. The resulting sheets of paper were fine, but lacked a certain depth.

A quick trip to the staff canteen and I had all the components I required: A melon for my head, cucumbers for my legs and arms. A whole turkey for my torso, mince and spaghetti for my internal organs and a carrot.

Taking the Xerox copies I had made earlier and a stapler, I added my perfectly copied features to the replica of me.

There was still one thing missing, however. I am famed throughout the land for my tee shirts and this finishing touch would be crucial if I were to get away with my deception. This was where I ran into my biggest problem. None of my hefty supply of tee shirts fitted the phoney 'James'.

It is for this reason that I contact you. Please can you rush me a (large or x-large) Xerox tee shirt? If you can, my freedom is ensured.

Waiting by the letterbox,

James Spence

To: James Spence
From: Xerox
Subject: Re: Duped

Good afternoon James and thank you very much for your very good and funny email!

I have actually got you a T-shirt that I will send to you in the post, in return we would like to see a picture of the finished article.

Please confirm that this is your correct mailing address and I will send it out to you.

You have given our office a nice little chuckle this afternoon.

Regards and best wishes

Lindsey

UK Internet Team

Tee Shirt

To: Airwick
From: James Spence
Subject: Home-Made Smells

Greetings Smell Producers,

I write to discuss with you the events that unfolded following my purchase of an Air Wick Crystal Air Design (Mystical Forest flavour) air freshener many moons ago.

I happen to live with a troublesome beast known throughout the civilised world as 'Angel the Cat'. Angel is a friendly, curious sort of feline, but has a tendency to create aromas which although natural, create an unholy stench capable of rendering a man unconscious at forty paces!

Since the purchase of the Air Wick Crystal Air Design (Mystical Forest flavour) air freshener, however, Angel's stink-factory has been somewhat neutralised. The only thing we smell now is in fact Mystical Forest. It's a nose treat and that's for sure!

My wife (Tiffany) and I (James) thought our days of retching and gagging were over. However, all good things must come to an end and after a very healthy length of time, the Mystical Forest eventually ran out of mystical power! The flat soon returned to its pre-Mystical Forest ways. Clothes pegs were a must!

Before long, our desire for more Mystical Forest was overwhelming! However, when we returned to our local supermarket, the Mystical Forest shelf was empty! The panic that ran through our faces must have been a sight to see, for we must've stared at that empty shelf for twenty full minutes, colour drained from our faces.

A heated discussion later and Tiffany and I arrived at a somewhat unusual solution: We decided to attempt to manufacture our own! If those Air Wick guys can do it, so can we. We live near a wood after all. It seemed almost too obvious a solution.

That night, as we stumbled through the rainy, unlit wood, Tiff and I endured many scratches and bruises as we picked up leaves, and forest debris to make our own air freshener. In our ingredient bucket we collected flowers, leaves, a small clump of mulch, straw, something brown, moss, grass, an avocado, something that looked a little like a bird's nest and (strangely) an unopened can of figs. Tragically, in our frantic search for components my favourite tee shirt (it had a photo of Belgium on the back) was destroyed.

Back at the house, we unceremoniously dumped our ingredients into the bath and soon started to mix up our Foresty brew. The thick brown sludge smelt alright, but it wasn't the pleasant mystical aroma of forest. It reminded Tiff of cabbage and me of parsnips. However, we decided to persevere, and left it to settle overnight.

During the night, our thick wet sludge did indeed settle. In fact, it formed a giant putrid smelling lump in the bath, which took 4 hours to chisel out. When we finally prised it out of the bath (still in one giant bath-shaped lump), we carried it (one at the front, one at the back) down to the supermarket to make a complaint about their failure to stock up on your wonderful air freshener. To our amazement, the air fresheners had arrived during the night and all our efforts were in vain. Of course, we parted with cash to restock!

I realise this story is a little unorthodox. My only regret is that I lost my favourite tee shirt during all the hubbub. It is for this reason that I write to you. As the heroes of the hour in this tale, I wondered if you had a (large) Air Wick tee shirt you could send my way?

Thanks very much for all you do. Our house smells lovely again and it's all down to you.

Many thanks

James Spence

RECKITT BENCKISER

Mr James Spence

Ref. 0001335850

2 September 2004

Dear Mr Spence

Thank you for your email dated 12 August 2004, which we received in our office regarding Airwick Crystal Air Mystical Forest.

We do apologise for the temporary lack of this product on your local supermarket shelf, and hope that Angel is behaving himself.

Thank you for contacting us on this matter.

Yours sincerely

S Willis

Sandie Willis
Consumer Services Department

Enc: Coupons £4.00

VOUCHERS TO THE VALUE OF £4.00

For all correspondence please write to: Reckitt Benckiser, PO Box 118, Clevedon, BS21 7ZH
Tel: 0845 7697079
Head office: Reckitt Benckiser (UK) Limited, Delta 1200, Welton Road, Delta Business Park, Swindon, Wiltshire SN5 7XZ
Registered Office: 103-105 Bath Road, Slough, Berkshire SL1 3UH Reg. No. 3982446

To:	Hellmann's
From:	James Spence
Subject:	Refreshing Mayo

Hi there,

I'm enjoying a nice cool glass of Hellmann's mayonnaise as we speak. I wondered if you had a tee shirt for a loyal fan and customer?

Thanks,

James Spence

To:	UGC Cinemas
From:	James Spence
Subject:	Cinemagic

Hi there Film Champions,

I love going to the cinema, and there are few cinemas better than a UGC cinema. Your cinema in Edinburgh is really great.

I write because of a tragic event that happened to me last time I was at your cinema.

Sebastian and I had decided to spend the evening at the pictures. He had decided to dress as a Mexican complete with sombrero and poncho. I had decided to wear my favourite tee shirt (it has an octopus on the back) and a bowler hat. We looked quite the thing as we sauntered into the foyer.

Having purchased our tickets from a particularly pleasant young lady, we made our way to the food counter. Sebastian, in keeping with his Mexican theme, ordered nachos. I ordered a large ice cream.

Before long it was time for our film to begin. Sebastian and I sat in our seats and prepared ourselves for a wonderful movie.

But before the film even began, disaster struck! The man in the seat behind Sebastian started demanding that he take off his Sombrero and I remove my bowler as his wife couldn't see the screen! Sebastian does not handle conflict well and kept quiet, but I, being the good diplomat, tried to reach a compromise. I knew Sebastian would never remove his sombrero, but I felt the furious couple may be persuaded to enjoy the film from a different seat.

The man did not take this suggestion well. He felt that since the cinema was largely empty and that since he and his good lady companion were there before us, that it was we who should move.

I could tell that Sebastian was feeling more and more distressed by the situation and so I needed to find some way to resolve this troublesome matter. The man and his wife were close to boiling point and Sebastian was becoming quite a bear!!

Suddenly I realised that this situation could be resolved one way and one way only: I proposed that we held a dance-off to decide who got to keep their seats. With the pre-movie music playing in the background, Sebastian started his crazed Mexican moves. At first he shimmied, then broke into a twist. A couple of back-flips later and I could tell the man was worried.

Much to my surprise, the man (who I secretly expected to be a dancing novice) broke into a moonwalk, followed by a foxtrot and ended with a slide across the floor. A crowd started to build up around us.

His wife was next onto the dance floor. Her body poppin' gyrations set the floor alight with a crazed dance energy.

It was all down to me. I knew in order to win the must-have seats, I'd have to dazzle with a pretty nifty dance move or two.

The following combination of moves was a remarkable sight. A skip, a prance, a jiggle and a hop later and the crowd were taking notice. Smoke was coming off my feet and steam was blasting out my ears. I twirled into a foxtrot, a tango and boogie. It was all leading to my final move, but I hadn't done the double-flip ultra back slide since the world disco contest 1989. With everything to play for, I switched into dance overload mode. I limbered up for the final move...

Taking a run down the isle towards the screen, I prepared for the ultimate manoeuvre. I felt the awe of the crowd, the wind in my bowler hat until...

My shirt got snagged on one of the seats and ripped, making me fall flat on my face.

Sebastian has not spoken to me since, and the couple got the pick of the seats.

Now I know that none of this is the UGC's fault. In fact I would recommend that no one attempts a dance-off in a cinema it's just the wrong venue altogether. However, my favourite shirt is forever gone.

I was therefore wondering if you happened to have a spare (large) UGC or promotional film tee shirt lying around that you may want to send to a loyal customer. I promise not to destroy it via the medium of dance.

Thanks for being a great cinema,

James "Dancin' Fool" Spence

Tel: 020 8987 5000
Fax: 020 8742 2998
email: info@ugccinemas.co.uk

05.11.04

Dear James,

I was very moved to hear how you ripped your favourite t-shirt whilst engaging in a dance off at UGC Edinburgh. I hope that this t-shirt and complimentary tickets will, in some small way, compensate you.

Yours Sincerely

Tim Hamlyn
UGC Cinemas Marketing

Tee Shirt and UGC Cinema Tickets

To: Boots
From: James Spence
Subject: It Must Be Chemistry

Hi there,

Over the years I cannot imagine how much money I have spent at Boots. I have always enjoyed and respected your company. Thank you for all your hard work. Biscuits all round!

How about some new lines in your stores, such as:

- In-store fortune telling. I know I'd cross your palms with silver!
- Free samples and in-store product trials (but obviously not the pills!)
- Actual Boots
- You have products for diabetics and slimmers, but what about those people who are trying to gain weight (wrestlers, pregnant women and men, etc)? You could offer 'double calorie' products (possibly deep fried)?

Anyway, it's your call. I wrote a poem in tribute to your fabulous company:

I like to shop at Boots. It thrills me to my soul.

Shampoo, toothpaste, nylons, and film (that's on a roll!)

With every single purchase, I do collect those points

Your service is terrific - it never disappoints!

The quality of your service, must be seen to be believed,

I like to look round a Boots store and I'm sad when I'm made to leave.

It's great to shop and to visit. Great items on every wall.

Well done you wonderful people. A pat on the head to you all!

I'd love a (large) Boots tee shirt? Have I earned one?

Thanks,

James Spence

Customer Care
PO Box 5300
Nottingham
NG90 1AA
Tel: 08450 70 80 90
Fax: 0115 959 5525
Minicom: 08450 70 80 91
Email: btc.cshelpdesk_team@boots.co.uk

Dear Mr Spence

Thanks for writing to me with your kind comments about Boots. I'm happy to hear you enjoy and respect our company. Thankyou very much for your poem it was very kind of you to put your feelings into words.

It is always really encouraging to receive ideas for new lines and complimentary letters such as yours and I have passed copies of your email on to the relevant teams.

I'm sorry but I do not have a Boots tshirt that I can send you but I have obtained two giftsets that I hope you will accept with my best wishes.

Thanks again for letting me know how you feel Mr Spence. If there is anything else I can do for you please let me know.

Yours sincerely

To:	Birds Eye
From:	James Spence
Subject:	Swimming the Blues

Hi there Fish Freezers,

I have a bizarre story to tell, but one that I'm confident you'd like to hear. It is an unusual tale, but I feel it is one that will amaze you to your very soul.

It must have been around half past ten in the evening. My wife (Tiffany), my good friend and house guest (Dr Sebastian), my cat (Angel) and I (me) were gathered around the television to enjoy several hours worth of Knots Landing videos. Dr Sebastian, who had until that moment seemed to enjoy the Knots Landing marathon, seemed to be getting a little quiet. He'd enjoyed the first eleven episodes, but perhaps twelve in a row was too many. Tiff had certainly passed out a few episodes back.

Anyway, it was around then that the penguins attacked. You heard me. Penguins. At first they threw stones, debris and pickled onions at the flat, but when that failed to grant them access to our home, they soon switched to their 'plan B'. The pesky black and white terrors had gathered together in a flock in an attempt to batter the door down. All the commotion awoke Tiff and she was not best pleased. "Why have the penguins picked our house for one of their 'raids'?" she (quite justifiably) asked. I had no answer.

Let me tell you, my Birdseye chums, when penguins attack your home, you become an animal. You have to protect your loved ones at all costs. Before long, I had thrown all our bombs and missiles at the penguins and had to resort to chucking the Knots Landing videos at the black and white icy devils. Dr Sebastian (my grizzly friend and long-term visitor) seemed to have gone into shock as he sat motionless on the sofa throughout our ordeal.

Luckily for us, I had plenty of Knots Landing videos to throw at the penguins (they made 344 episodes plus the reunion special) but even with that healthy supply, like the show itself, the episodes came to an abrupt end. Tiff immediately looked to my Doctor Who DVDs, but we both knew I'd rather be pecked to death by penguins than live without my Doctor Who collection.

A large penguin broke in through the front window squirting milkshake everywhere. Some of it got onto my favourite tee shirt (it had the Supremes on it), ruining it forever. It was the first major loss of what the history books might call 'Battle Penguin'.

The cat had managed to p-p-p-pick off a few of them, but the little black and white villains kept coming. I sent Tiff into the kitchen to look for other items we could use to defend ourselves, and she opened up the fridge. This, my good buddies, was the turning point in our struggle.

You see, the reason we had penguin troubles was instantly obvious to her (she's a smarty-pants). We'd just visited our fantastic local supermarket and had bought some exceptionally tasty-looking Birdseye frozen fish (I call it a fishcicle). The penguins must've seen us making the purchase and followed us home from the store to get their grubby flippers on our 'denizens of the deep'.

There was only one thing for it. Tiff reached for the frying pan and fried up those fishy treats. Man, were they tasty! Once consumed, we showed the penguins our empty plates. They looked tearfully at each other, realising that the delicious bounty was gone, and shuffled off back to the South Pole.

I can't blame Birdseye for anything that happened that crazy night. Heck, it's really a tribute to you that your fish is so tasty. However at the end of this story, I find myself down one (Supremes) tee shirt. Tiff suggested that before I break down into 'one of my spasms' over the loss of the tee shirt, I should contact you to see if you happen to have a (large) Birdseye tee shirt (or equivalent) to take its place. If so, you'd make me a happy chappy indeed.

Here's to you, Birdseye, and thanks for all the fish,

James Spence

Birds Eye Consumer Care
Freepost NATE139
Milton Keynes
MK9 1BR

Freephone: 0800 332277
Minicom: 0800 0280173
www.birdseye.co.uk

Ref: 461108
Date: 5 January 2005

Mr J Sp[illegible] 461108

Dear Mr Spence

I was delighted to learn how pleased you are with our Birds Eye Captain's Fish Fingers and the great story about the penguins.

We spend a great deal of time and effort in trying to create products that deliver great results and that our consumers will enjoy using, so it is always nice to receive such positive feedback.

I will make sure your comments are passed on to the marketing manager concerned and I am sure they will be delighted to get your feedback.

Naturally I hope you will continue to enjoy using our Birds Eye Captain's Fish Fingers, I have enclosed some Birds Eye vouchers and if you want to pass these to your neighbour so they can purchase some of the fish fingers and then they can attack their house.

I have made an enquiry to see if we have any spare large Birds Eye t-shirts, as soon as I hear from the relevant department I will then contact you.

Once again thank you for the wonderful story and I will contact you again in due course.

Yours sincerely

Kevin Hudson
Consumer Care Advisor

--
Enclosures:
2 x Birds Eye Coupon £3

VOUCHERS TO THE VALUE OF £3.00

The Captain's on a Nutrition Mission!

If you have access to the Internet and would like to receive exciting product news, special offers and competitions from Birds Eye, please visit www.birdseye.co.uk to register your details.

Unilever Ice Cream & Frozen Food Limited Registered Office: Station Avenue, Walton-on-Thames, Surrey, KT12 1NT Registered in England & Wales No.343496

To:	Delonghi
From:	James Spence
Subject:	Hobbin' Around

Hi there,

I love Delonghi products like you would not believe. I have just bought a Delonghi Oven and Hob, inspired by the wonderful Delonghi toaster we received for our wedding last year. Oh Delonghi, how do you make such stylish kitchen items? What is your secret? Wait! I know the answer already hard work.

Ever since we got the new hob, my wife (Tiffany) and I have cooked some great meals. We've enjoyed Chicken Fajitas, Chicken Tikka Marsala, Chicken Pasta Bake, Chicken Fried Rice, Chicken in Black Bean Sauce, Chicken Madras, Chicken in Ice Cream Sauce, Chicken stuffed with sprouts, Chicken Marzipan and Chicken (on it's own as we had run out of sauce). As you may have guessed by now, we keep chickens, or at least we did until we got our Delonghi.

I want to shout from the rooftops how wonderful my Delonghi is, but sadly due to a condition my doctors call 'chicken throat', I cannot shout. All I can do is make a buck, buck sound. I therefore wondered if I could endorse your products by wearing a Delonghi tee shirt. Do such things exist? I would LOVE one if they do. What say you, my good buddies?

Cockadoodledoo, amigos!!!

James Spence

To: Starbucks
From: James Spence
Subject: Coffee Conundrum

Greetings Coffeehounds,

Is there anything you guys can't do? I think I've tried every single item on the Starbucks menu board! Even the tea! I think your coffee shops are simply touched by inspiration.

My good friend and fellow coffee drinker Dr Sebastian consumes coffee and chocolate until he is stuffed! And even though Dr Sebastian and I often argue quite heatedly, we've never been asked to leave because of our enthused debates yet.

One day, whilst drinking coffee in one of your delightful lounges, the good doctor and I thought up a few new coffee recipes, which we later decided to try out. Please see the attached list (we actually made these and tried them, and have posted our comments below):

- Strawberry coffee: We fused Coffee with the delights of Strawberry jam. It was a little gloopy and had strawberry chunks in it. Revolting.
- Brandy chocachinno: Brandy and chocolate. Now that's what I call a treat. Dr Sebastian had a couple of these.
- Prune juice espresso: The juice drained from prunes mixed in with the coffee. I must say I rather liked this one, but Dr Sebastian claimed it gave him the 'tummy wibbles'
- Mint Cappuccino: Now this is one we both agreed on. It was lovely. We simply popped a ground-up mint into the bottom of the cup before preparing the coffee. It really made for a tasty cup. When we later tried it with toothpaste, it was rank.
- Whiskey and Vodka Coffee: Now here was one the Dr and I both enjoyed tremendously. We had several of these

in fact before continuing with our experiments.

- Oatmeal frapuccino: It was better than we'd expected.
- Rum tea: I must admit, there wasn't much tea in it, but it was very nice indeed.
- Fish-finger Surprise: The main surprise was how revolting this one was.
- Salt-lick Macchiato: A lick of salt, prior to drinking the coffee. Required a few shots of port to get over this one.
- Dr Sebastian's 'Mystery' Brew: I don't know what was in it, but it was excellent. It reminded me a little of digestive biscuits and tequila
- Kebab and chilli sauce: We had gone out for a kebab by this stage. It was very tasty, but contained no coffee.

I don't know if our experiments are of any value to you. Either way, it was a wonderful night in.

As I am a huge fan of your coffee-lounges, I wondered if you had a (large) Starbucks tee shirt you could send me? I'd be most grateful.

Thanks ever so,

James Spence

Starbucks Coffee Company (UK) Limited
11 Heathmans Road
Parsons Green
London SW6 4TJ
telephone 020 7878 4900
facsimile 020 7731 6534

Our ref: 163273

Mr James Spence

16 August 2004

Dear Mr Spence

Once again thank you for taking the time and energy to share your thoughts with Starbucks Coffee Company.

As promised, please find enclosed complimentary beverage vouchers as a token of my appreciation.

I hope you will continue to enjoy our coffee for years to come, even the uniquely customised options!

Kind regards

Daniel Forsythe
Customer Care Specialist

Starbucks Coffee Company (UK) Limited

Registered Office
11 Heathmans Road
Parsons Green
London SW6 4TJ

Registered No
2959325

To:	Clairol
From:	James Spence
Subject:	Kiss and Make-up

Dear Clairol,

My wife (Tiffany) loves Clairol products. She uses them every day and recommends them to all her friends.

I wondered if there was any way I could save a few quid by making your products at home. Please could you send me instructions on how to do this and provide details of any equipment I might need. I already have a bucket and spoon to mix it all together.

Alternatively, if you're worried about me taking this information to start up my own company, perhaps you could reward Tiffany's loyalty by sending her a free Clairol tee shirt (or vouchers for Clairol stuff - she'd love that too).

And while we're at it, give yourselves a congratulatory slap on the back for being such a great company.

Many thanks,

James Spence

To:	Findus
From:	James Spence
Subject:	Oven Nice Day

Dear Findus,

I write to tell a strange tale. A bizarre tale. A tale you may not believe. A tale of awe and wonder. A tale of desperation, drama, crisis and frozen food.

It was two days ago, 'Hat Day' in the peaceful neighbourhood of Cairneyhill, Fife. I had put the finishing touches to my own hat, a large mahogany Easter Bonnet, and had just put my chainsaw away having carved the fine detail beautifully.

"Fetch me my supper," I demanded of my wife, Tiffany.

"No," she responded, with anger, "if you want eats, you can jolly well get them yourself. I've had a busy day at work, while you've squandered the day carving a ridiculous hat, heavier than a portable television."

"Look, honey," I began, "I've just spent three hours hard at work and, as such, have no energy left for dinner encookment. Besides which, I have never cooked before in my life, and wouldn't know where to begin!"

Tiffany shrugged and went back to her day-dreams of driving a bus, leaving me with a serious dinner dilemma.

There was nothing for it. With a sigh, I resigned myself to the fact that I was going to have to make my own dinner, and to make matters worse, I had already put the chainsaw away. I was on my own, with no goons or henchmen to help me out. Absorbing this information, I immediately made my way to the kitchen and found a device that I had heard Tiffany refer to on many occasions as the 'fridge'. Opening it up, I was greeted by numerous foodstuffs of all different colours (except blue).

I immediately grabbed the first items I could find, which I later learned the names of: a jar of 'mayonnaise', an 'egg', some 'lard', another 'egg', a 'shoe' and three 'grapes'. These ingredients, I mixed together in a bucket and roasted over a bonfire I made in the middle of the kitchen.

When the Fire Brigade had calmed the flames, I tasted the charred black lump that I had produced.

When I got out of hospital, I returned to what was left of my home and decided that the 'fridge' idea had been a mistake. Instead I turned to the 'freezer'. Inside which, was a 'Findus Three Cheeses Crispy Pancake'. Just as I was about to take a bite, I realised that there was packaging to be removed first, and then the item had to be heated. This I was able to do with a blowtorch, with only one small mishap in which my favourite tee shirt (depicting a bear in a poncho) was engulfed in flames.

The 'Findus Three Cheeses Crispy Pancake' was delicious and I consumed it with the knowledge that I had earned it. I had cooked it from scratch with my own bare hands (and blowtorch). And with my new found skills, I'm now considering opening my own restaurant, and it's all thanks to you.

So, I just wanted to write to thank you for a delicious dinner. I also wondered if you had any Findus goodies, such as a (large) Findus tee shirt to replace the one I lost making the meal.

Many thanks and keep up the great work,

James Spence

PS If you have a 'Findus' neck brace, that would be great, as my neck is too frail to support a mahogany headpiece.

Mr J Spence

0704037666A 25 October 2004

Dear Mr Spence,

Thank you very much for recently contacting Findus Consumer Services regarding your success with Findus Three Cheese Crispy Pancakes.

We were also pleased to hear of your hat making intricacies and we hope the hat day went off without any problems. We also hope your wife's dream of bus driving bears fruit, Findus Crispy Pancakes have been popular throughout the nation for many years and also come in Minced Beef and Chicken, Bacon & Sweetcorn varieties which you may like to try.

I would suggest however that the more conventional cooking methods would give a better result, e.g. grilling or oven cooking. Unfortunately at this moment in time we do not have any T Shirts, but I have enclosed a Findus cap which you may find useful. I think you will find this slightly lighter than a small portable television.

Thank you once again for your interest in Findus and we hope you continue to enjoy our products.

Yours sincerely

R. Steele

Rob Steele
Technical Officer - Consumer Services

Findus Consumer Services
www.findus.co.uk

Registered in Eng... 3463 8785 ...ucester Road, Redhill, Surrey, RH1 1FD

To: Goodyear
From: James Spence
Subject: Goodyear? Greatyear More Like!

Dear the Staff of the Goodyear Blimp,

I am a man obsessed with the Goodyear Blimp. From morning until night I think about how fantastic it must be to ride in. Sometimes I even daydream about owning the Goodyear Blimp! Just imagine turning up for work and having to park it on the roof! That would certainly set us apart from the other abattoirs.

The other week when I was out wrestling, I happened to mention to my good friend and houseguest Sebastian that it would be pretty cool to own the Goodyear Blimp. The conversation moved on and I didn't think anything more of it until Monday, when I turned up at my house and Sebastian had spent the day in the shed knocking up his own version of the Blimp out of poly bags, Velcro and muzzles.

This morning I flew it to work. Let me tell you, it attracted many admiring glances, but I dare say it didn't turn half as many heads as the real blimp would. And you know what? I was the envy of everyone at work, until they sacked me for muzzle embezzlement.

Given that I'm now unemployed, I wondered if my devotion to the Goodyear Blimp could be rewarded with a Goodyear tee shirt? It would make my day! I'd be happy to trade you a few muzzles for it.

Thanks a million Goodyear and well done on some great products and blimps!

Hugs,

James Spence

To: Kleenex
From: James Spence
Subject: Achoo!

Hey Dudes,

So I get up one day and I'm looking in the mirror, thinking to myself what's up with the world? There's cruelty, poverty, hate, aggression, gherkins and depression out there. It's a sad story. I wish I could stay in my house all the time. Then it hits me - WHAM - there's a way I COULD stay in my house all the time. Read on, my friends for the tale about to be revealed will fill you with awe and wonder...

Looking around my house for ingredients, I immediately set to work building a clone of myself who could go out into the world in my place (i.e. he could do my job, get my shopping, get my haircuts, etc.) It was difficult at first, because I could only use the things I happened to have lying around my house, but believe it or not I had everything I required: bread, bananas, ping pong balls, loudspeakers, some carpet, a giant sausage, all my knowledge on a CD ROM, ten human fingers, an unopened can of tuna and of course some Kleenex. I soon assembled my clone.

I recall the moment I gave him life with some fondness. Lightning crashed outside and thunder roared through the sky. Staring at the lifeless body of my clone (I call him Barney), I asked myself 'Do I have the right to do this?', then thought, 'maybe' and inserted a couple of batteries. His eyes clunked open and he looked at me standing over him. He sat upright and said 'hey dude what's up man?' and we both had a can of beer and a bit of a sit down.

He was nearly perfect...

The only problem I faced was that my clone had no tee shirt. You may think, heck that's not much of a problem for a dude who is capable of building and giving life to a clone of himself, but you my friend would be incorrect. You see, I'm known throughout the land for my collection of tee shirts and this vital final component would be critical if I were pull off my deception.

I therefore turn to you, my Kleenex friends. You could well become the heroes of this strange and (I confess) a little unorthodox tale. If you happen to have a spare (large) Kleenex tee shirt, my lifetime of lounging around the house can begin, and Barney will not have to walk around topless.

Thanks very much, dudes. Thanks for all your hard work making Kleenex one of the few good things the outside world has to offer.

Thanks a million, heroes,

James Spence

15 November 2004

Mr. James Spence

Dear Mr. Spence,

Thank you for contacting Kimberly-Clark Corporation. We appreciate the opportunity to respond to your request for a donation.

Because our products and our company have become so well known over the years, we have been invited to assist in many fine programs and projects. Although we would certainly like to help, the volume of requests is simply too great to accommodate.

We are sorry to inform you that we do' nt have any Kleenex T-shirts available.

Please accept the Kleenexvoucher with our best wishes.
We did like your story..

Thank you again for your interest in our products and for taking the time to contact us.

Yours sincerely,

Edith Willson

Edith Willson
Consumer Services Department

001226907A

Kimberly-Clark

Kimberly-Clark Consumer Services
1 Tower View, Kings Hill, West Malling, Kent ME19 4

To:	Intel
From:	James Spence
Subject:	What's Inside?

Hi there Guys,

I was sitting around the other day when I suddenly thought of the funniest thing in the world! Ever.

What if you printed tee shirts that said 'Intel inside'?!! I nearly crapped myself laughing.

It would imply that the wearer of the tee shirt, would themselves contain an Intel chip.

If by any chance you have these, PLEASE can you send me one (large). I would wear it every day (as long as I didn't die laughing).

James Spence

To: George Foreman
From: James Spence
Subject: Penguin Story

Hi George

I write to tell you how great my George 'Lean Mean Fat Grilling Machine' is. I use it on a regular basis and it always produces great results. You are quite the engineer.

Several weeks back, I had to defend my home from a group of intruders all dressed in black and white, with flippers. We fought them off the property, and the 'George Foreman' played a part. That's right! You see, we had been infested with penguins (it's rare, but in Scotland, we sometimes get penguins coming into the house looking for fish). This was the case recently.

At first we tried to 'shoo' them away by hurtling video cassettes at them, then when they had run out, we searched the house for other ammunition. It was at this point we realised that they smelt the fish we had bought at a supermarket recently. My wife whipped out the George Foreman Grill, fried the fish up and we scoffed the lot! Let me tell you, it was good fish, but we ate it very fast granting ourselves the tummy wibbles, but that's a whole other story.

Unfortunately during the penguin attack, my favourite tee shirt (it had Diana Ross and the Supremes on it) was covered in milk-shake, ruining it forever. It was a sad loss to my wardrobe.

Anyway, once the fish was gone, the penguins soon wandered out of the house. Perhaps one day, we'll invade their home to see how they like it!!

Anyway, I just thought you'd like to know how your grill saved our home from penguin attack. I also wondered if you happened to have a (large) George Foreman tee shirt which you could send me to replace my Diana Ross one?

Thanks a million George.

Love the Grill,

James Spence

To:	Oddbins
From:	James Spence
Subject:	A Spiritual Experience

Dear Oddbins Customer Service Team,

Several years back, whilst on a trip to Glasgow, I saw a most remarkable thing outside of an Oddbins store, and now feel I have to write to tell you about it, as it has haunted me ever since. Oh why won't the nightmares stop?

It was a cold winter's evening (July the 17th of September, to be exact). My shopping expedition for Valentine's gifts had gone well and I had picked up all the items on my list: Koala seeds, test tubes, creamed snouts, electrodes and a water bed. I was happy in the knowledge that my wife (Tiffany) would have a most memorable day, as long as my experiments were a success and I could deliver Buddy the Koala-Pig as promised.

However, my mood rapidly changed outside of Oddbins (Dundee), when I observed, coming out of the store, what could only be described as: a yeti!

The yeti was a strange beast to see. For one thing he had no head. He was, however, tall like a sparrow, fat like a whippet, furry like a gecko and had tusks and a wooden spike made of metal coming from his head.

The beast observed me for a while, watching my unusual dances of greeting, before taking flight down a side street. Realising that a Yeti would make an ideal Christmas gift (at that time Christmas was just a month away), I followed the trail the yeti had left behind (a soft pink crunchy powder-liquid, only blue and hard). Soon, I had caught up with him and he high-fived me for my perseverance.

Of course, the story does not end here, otherwise I would be famous as 'the guy who caught the yeti outside Edinburgh Oddbins'. No, the sneaky furry bald devil had a trick up his sleeve: the mind scrambler, a sort-of laser-guided ray knife, which he immediately set to work on my brain, and worse, my favourite tee shirt (it had a picture of a carnivorous dinosaur, vegetarian, on it).

I was lucky to have escaped with my life.

I write to you now to tell of the amazing events that happened to me. As a loyal fan and customer I also write to ask if you happened to have a large Oddbins tee shirt that you could send me to replace the one I lost on that warm Summer night last January.

Many thanks, and please warn your Aberdeen staff that there's still a yeti loose in the city!

Keep up the brilliant work, and thanks a million for making every trip to Oddbins a great adventure,

James Spence

To: Hovis
From: James Spence
Subject: Proposing a Toast

I love Hovis Bread. It really is the best bread out there. I just wanted to write and let you know that all your hard work in those bakeries is appreciated by Joe Public (i.e. me!)

I wrote a little poem (you may wish to use this in an advertising campaign or staff newsletter?)

Hovis makes the best bread. It's great to have a slice.
I stuff it in my mouth and boy does it taste nice!
Of all the bread that's out there, it's Hovis I like most,
I like it as a sandwich, I love it as my toast.
When I write my shopping list, Hovis is a must.
Thanks, you Hovis bakers, for the way you earn your crust!

Any chance of a Hovis t-shirt for a loyal fan?

Thanks,

James Spence

British Bakeries Limited
Head Office
King Edward House
PO Box 527
King Edward Court
Windsor, Berkshire
SL4 1TJ England

Telephone +44 (0)1753 857123
Facsimile +44 (0)1753 791739

www.britishbakeries.co.uk

Mr J Spence

29 September 2004

Our ref.: C3505ML

Dear Mr Spence,

May I take this opportunity to apologise for the delay in returning your enquiry. We do our very best to deal with all the enquiries that we receive, but as you may appreciate the volume tends to sometimes delay the response.

Thank you so much for your very kind comments and poem. It is always so good to hear from our consumers especially when the comments are favorable ones. I will of course let you know should we use your poem in any capacity

Thank you for taking the time to write to us and by way of an apology for the lengthy delay in returning this enquiry please find the enclosed vouchers and a little token of gratitude

With Kindest Regards,

HOVIS

Granary

THANK YOU
HOVIS
SILLY
BEGGAR

SCRABBLE

To:	Domino's
From:	James Spence
Subject:	Spotted

Greetings Domino's Divas,

I wanted to write to you to say how much I appreciate Domino's pizzas. You guys really bailed me out of a bad situation and you probably didn't even know it. The following story is strange, but don't let the weirdness distract you from the truth.

I had bought a grand piano on the Internet and put the cheque in a stamped envelope that I then carried to the post box, located near a Domino's pizza. As I arrived at the pillar-box, I noticed, to my surprise, the door had been left open. Clearly some an absent-minded (drunk?) postman hadn't been doing his job correctly. Fear not, a strongly worded email has already gone out to address that particular issue.

There was also a trail of biscuits on the ground leading inside the post box. To cut a long story short, I ended up stuffed full of biscuits, but alas locked inside the pillar-box.

I shouted for help for a long time, but no one came, until after several hours, an old man finally spotted my predicament. He asked if he could be of any help and I told him that I was quite comfortable but hungry. He said he would get me something to eat.

Two hours later and he returned with a live turkey, and asked if that would do. I explained that as I was trapped in a pillar-box, I could neither kill, pluck, cook or indeed eat the turkey and that it would be preferable for him to bring me something ready to eat and flat enough to fit in the letterbox.

You've probably worked out where this is going my friends. Yes, Domino's came to the rescue and several delicious slices were passed in to me. Unfortunately in the dark, I spilt tomato, egg and pilchards down the front of my favourite tee shirt (it had a picture of a goat eating underpants on it).

Eventually, I was released from my postal prison, but alas my tee shirt was forever ruined. Domino's came to my rescue on that day, and I write to enquire whether you could come to my rescue once more. Do you have a large Domino's tee shirt you could send to a persistent pizza punter? I would be thrilled to wear it, as I LOVE Domino's pizza.

Thanks so much. It's always a pleasure to visit Domino's and well done on having such great staff.

Waiting by the letter box (although not literally this time),

James Spence

To: Vauxhall
From: James Spence
Subject: An Out of this World Driving Experience

Hi there,

I drive a Corsa which I enjoy so much, I call myself a Vaux-a-hallic! Yes, it is a fab car. However, whilst driving it a few weeks back some strange things happened which I felt I had to write and let you know about.

My wife (Tiffany) and I were out for a late-night drive towards our local wood, in search of ingredients for a new smell we were working on. We arrived there safely and comfortably and were able to pick up an assortment of components to create the forest smells we craved.

We opened up the (spacious) boot and put in the various flowers, twigs, figs and leaves. Out of the blue, we heard a strange sound coming from above. Tiff looked up (I looked to the left because I have a poor sense of direction, but the wife soon adjusted my head to face the correct way). I could not believe my eyes. Above our heads was what could only be described as a spacecraft. Yowza!

It lowered itself down in front of us and a moist little man with a beak and horns got out, asking us to take him to our leader. I immediately thought of my good friend and house guest Dr Sebastian. He'd surely know what to do.

The creature got into the back of the Corsa and commented on how roomy it was back there. He admired the quality craftsmanship of the inside of the car and apologised for secreting a foul smelling gel-like substance on our upholstery.

Back at the house, Dr Sebastian was introduced to the funny little man. He seemed uncommonly quiet as the little man performed his 'dance of greetings' which involved juggling our cat (Angel) and doing unspeakable acts to my favourite tee shirt (it has a sub-atomic moose on the front). Needless to say the shirt was ruined. I have the worst luck with tee shirts!

The alien stayed just long enough for a few quick games of wrestling and head slaps, before making his excuses. We took him back to his craft (again he was most impressed with the Corsa).

Before the ship took flight, the little creature said "Thank you for making me feel welcome. Your luxury car has convinced me that this world is a good world and I have decided not to invade. Sorry about your tee shirt."

It was a truly remarkable tale. The only down side of the whole story is the tee shirt that was lost during the creature's greeting dance. It is for this reason I write. As a way of treasuring the warm memory of the night Vauxhall and I saved the world, I wondered if you could send me a (large) Vauxhall tee shirt to replace the one I lost that night?

Thanks very much. I love my Corsa,

James Spence

To: James Spence
From: Vauxhall
Subject: Re: An Out of this World Driving Experience

Thank you for your recent email and I was so sorry to learn of the accidental damage caused to your Vauxhall teeshirt during your recent woodland expedition. I can certainly appreciate your disappointment.

As requested, I am sending under separate cover, a replacement Vauxhall teeshirt, and have taken the liberty of enclosing, in the same envelope, some Network Q air fresheners.

Whilst apologising that the fresheners may not be of the "forest fragrance" variety favoured by yourself and your wife, I would recommend that to keep the new teeshirt in optimum condition, you remain INSIDE your treasured Corsa whilst wearing it, and sniff the delicate aroma of coconut and vanilla.

These air fresheners have proved very popular with our customers so we hope the aroma will grow on you, though not literally of course, as coconut/vanilla stains on a Vauxhall teeshirt would not look quite the ticket.

As per the instructions on the freshener packets, please avoid direct contact between freshener and textiles/ plastic? ie. do not affix them to the dashboard or have them touching any other plastic/textile part of the car. Replacing a teeshirt is not a problem, but replacing your vehicle's dashboard, could prove a little trickier.

The teeshirt is on its way, although regrettably, by red Post Office van rather than space-craft. I trust this suggested course of action is acceptable. Thank you for allowing me to assist.

Kind regards

G Pooley (Mrs)

CUSTOMER CARE CENTRE

Tee Shirt and Air Fresheners
Who makes sure your used car smells as fresh as the day you bought it?
NETWORKQ
Number one for used cars.

To:	Borders Books
From:	James Spence
Subject:	Keep Your Spirits Up!

Greetings to you, the Staff at Borders,

The other day, when I was out bustin' ghosts, I happened into one of your fine outlets in pursuit of a fiendishly foul phantom. The spooky spectre had been hassling decent people in the Fort Kinnaird Retail Park, Edinburgh and causing quite a commotion with his unearthly and uncanny manner. As it happens, I'm feared throughout the underworld, and when the abhorrent apparition spotted me, that's when he attempted to 'hide out' in Borders. The good people of Fort Kinnaird were terrified, but when they saw my equipment, they swiftly realised a professional was on the case. Read on my friends, for the next few paragraphs will blow your minds!

My bustin' briefcase held: garlic, a wooden stake, silver bullets, a magic herring, a rolled up newspaper, a live squirrel in a cardboard box, three pictures of Keith Richards at different stages in his career and a flask of tea in case I got thirsty. That briefcase has got me out of some scrapes I don't mind admitting, and as you'll soon find out, today was no exception. Oh yes, I had all the tools I could ever need to track down, catch and dispose of even the most terrifying of foes: Clawbeak, the Ragin' Freak of Death. But luckily, Clawbeak was nowhere to be found in this tale. Hey! Why not move your eyes down a paragraph? That's where the story continues after all!

As I stealthily tracked the naughty spirit through Borders, I noticed your fantastic range of newspapers and magazines, books, calendars, CDs and DVDs and an impressive range of other quality goods. What a shop! It was almost enough to distract me from the mysterious fiend wandering the store, but you forget, I'm a professional. Yes, after only the briefest of browses through the magazine section, I returned to the task at hand. Using a device of my own invention: the Ghost-track 500 (much better than all 499 of its predecessors), I identified where the brute was hiding. You guessed it wise ones, amongst the romance novels. Carefully, I sneaked up to the 'passion shelves' and peeked around the corner to where the fearsome creature lurked. My worst fears were confirmed. It was a gnome.

With lightning reflexes, I reached for the bustin' briefcase and produced my flask of tea. A sip of the warm stuff later, and I had concocted an ingenious plan. There's only one thing a gnome hates, and that's wearing tee shirts. They feel they're a bit too informal and make their hats look silly. Armed with this vital piece of knowledge, I quietly slipped off my favourite tee shirt (it had a picture of a bucking horse on it), and threw it over the gnome. Want to know what happened next? Then check out the next few sentences.

The gnome went into spasm. He thrashed around on the floor for a good eighteen minutes, then after tiring himself out, imploded, taking my tee shirt and any evidence that this story actually happened with him. The thorough little monster even performed that old gnome trick of erasing his existence from the memories of all he had met. It was only I who was left with the burden of that day (my mind was shielded by the impenetrable Keith Richard's pictures).

So you see, my friends, I have quite the tale to tell and the only evidencc I can offer is that there is now a gaping hole in my tee shirt collection. If there were such a thing as a free (large or extra large) Borders tee shirt, I would be thrilled and would consider it fair payment for the removal of a gnome from Borders (Edinburgh branch).

I always enjoy visiting my local Borders. Well done on a great store. You guys rule supreme!

James Spence

BORDERS

James,

Unfortunately that darn gnome has taken all our Borders T-shirts! But have given you a couple of other ones by way of a Thank You!

and hope you keep coming back to keep us safe from those gnomes!

Carolyn.

With Compliments

To:	Sheetz
From:	James Spence
Subject:	What Do You Do?

Hi there,

I have never heard of your company, but I stumbled across your web site, and it is a beauty. Please can you send me details of what your company does and a free tee shirt (large).

Thanks,

James Spence

To:	Merrydown
From:	James Spence
Subject:	Slurp

Hi there Cider-makers!

I love Merrydown cider. The very thought of it fills me with joy. It's the most filling and refreshing drink out there. I love to enjoy a glass of your cider whilst surfing the web, in fact, I am doing so right now. Cheers!

I wrote a poem about your cider to celebrate how darned tasty it is:

The first time I tried Merrydown was a delightful day.
When I sipped its flavour, I didn't know what to say.
I smiled as it went down my throat, so happy was I then.
I had to grab another glass and knock one back again.
The first time I drank Merrydown, my life became complete.
Its apples made me happy from my head down to my feet.
When I have a day at work, I come home in disgust,
And head towards my fridge because that cider is a must!

Do you have a (large) t-shirt for a HUGE Merrydown fan?

Keep up the superb work,

James Spence

To: James Spence
From: Merrydown
Subject: Re: Slurp

Dear James -

Thanks for your e mail, its always good to hear from stalwarts. I will try and dig out a T shirt, but it will be a Merry Down one not a Vintage one!

Cheers,

Chris

Managing Director - Cider Division

To:	O'Brien's
From:	James Spence
Subject:	Snacks for the Memory

Hi there,

I have just finished a very tasty lunch and I wanted to write to tell you about it (note: this is for your information only and not to be shared with any penguins).

The story begins with my wife (Tiffany) and I (James) being unable to decide what to eat for lunch. We had a busy morning infiltrating government buildings and collating information on possible future penguin attacks. Let me tell you, it's hungry work keeping one step ahead of the black and white blighters.

We stopped off at our local O'Brien's and I ordered a tuna wrappo. Tiff had the Chicken and Bacon triple-decker. As usual, we identified the seat with the clearest view of all entrances and exits. When we were finally confident no one had followed us in, we allowed ourselves to relax a little and soak up the enjoyable atmosphere in the restaurant.

When the delightful serving wench brought our food to the table, we were hot dog mighty king kong impressed. Not only did it smell good, but it was wonderfully presented too. At first bite, the tastes were titillating, tickling and taunting my taste buds. The second sent sensual signals up my synapses. But disaster struck on bite number three when the door burst open and in came wave after wave of penguins. Somehow the South Pole citizens had tracked us down. That's the last time I order tuna!

Fortunately I had a killer whale in my bag, allowing us the distraction we needed to get away with our lives, our lunches and our love of O'Briens food.

The story does end happily in that we escaped with our lives, but at the back of my mind there is a bitter taste. Somehow the penguins had found us in your cafe. It is for this reason I write. If I had an O'Briens tee shirt, I could easily 'hide out' in your restaurants whenever I got peckish, and those devilish penguins would never track me down. So my good O'Briens friends, do you have a tee shirt for a loyal fan and customer?

Either way, keep up the excellent work and well done to everyone for making yours a fantastic organisation (and especially well done to the staff at my local O'Briens - Dunfermline).

Happy sandwich making,

James Spence

To:	Somerfield
From:	James Spence
Subject:	Tee Shirt Free Zone

Dear Somerfield Customer Service Staff,

I write to report a matter of the gravest significance, and I'm afraid it concerns the conduct of one of your members of staff. Normally every visit to Somerfield is met with enthusiasm and warmth. The staff are always polite and friendly and it is a pleasure to spend my time perusing your store, buying much needed food or even just hiding in the freezers. However, this high standard is clearly difficult to maintain, as I discovered to my horror! The member of staff in question is not one of the many attentive staff who work on the shop floor of your excellent supermarkets, but another member of your staff. A, shall we say, 'moving' person. Yes, the following tale is one of woe and regret. Read on compadres, read on...

It was a bitter Monday morning and I, like so many others, was navigating through busy traffic en route to the place of my employment. Bleary eyed and miserable, I weaved in and out of a particularly heavy traffic marmalade (it's thicker than a traffic jam). As a nosey parker it is my duty to look inside the other vehicles and study the faces of my fellow travellers. On this particular Monday, they were grey, drawn and bitter. Their journeys were clearly as arduous as my own.

A cold drizzle pattered against my windscreen, not enough to necessitate my wipers on permanently, but too much to leave them off altogether. The thick atmosphere has transformed my hair into a half-afro (a halfro?). My car's arial had been snapped off through the night and I had no music to lighten my mood and the smell of stale cigarettes clung to my jacket from a weekend's over-indulgence at the local boozer. And then Somerfield entered my life.

In the slow moving lane of traffic to my left, I noticed a Somerfield lorry. It was moving as one would expect in time with the traffic and was also obeying the Highway code. I cannot fault the driving skills of the man at the helm. However, when, by chance, I happened to glance at the face of the driver, I was shocked to see that he was committing the ultimate Monday morning driving sin.

He was smiling.

Perhaps he was feeling smug because of the incredibly low prices of the goods he hauled? Maybe he was feeling self-satisfied on account of the quality of his wares? Or perhaps he was just excited because he worked for the best darned supermarket out there? I don't know and I guess I will never know. All I can tell you is that it made me sizzle!!

I wondered if there was any way that this psychological damage could be repaired via the gift of a free Somerfield tee shirt to an unwavering and adorable customer?

Anyway, just wanted to drop you a note to say well done on providing a great service.

Many thanks,

James Spence

To:	James Spence
From:	Somerfield
Subject:	Re: Tee Shirt Free Zone

Or should that say Free Tee Shirt Zone?

Either way we found your e-mail very entertaining James, thank you for taking the time to write it.

Unfortunately we are fresh out of tee shirts at the moment, but the minute we get some in stock (which should be in a couple of weeks time) we'll be in touch to find out where you'd like one sent.

Thanks again for spreading the lorry drivers smile..

Regards,

Zoe

To: Gossard
From: James Spence
Subject: Pants

Greetings Bra and Knicker-makers,

I'm a man and must confess that I have personally never used your products! Well, maybe one time on holiday in Rio, but I was very drunk and needed the money. I digress. Your products are very well respected by my wife, Tiffany, who loves to wear them (almost) every day.

We put our heads together and came up with a few ideas you may like to try out:

- Gossard man-pants: Underwear for a man with the same push-up technology that gets used on the ladies.
- Gossard scented undies (available in the following smells): Pine, Mint and Praline
- Socks: There's nothing more sexy than a woman in the right pair of socks!
- Breath mints

We both love your company. Do you have a (large) tee shirt for a loyal fan and many-time customer?

Thanks,

James Spence

To: Shell
From: James Spence
Subject: Bus-ted

Dear Shell,

Do you own a bus? I do. I own a bus. That's right, me. A bus. Owned.

You see I like to start every letter with a memorable fact. If ever you wanted to know something about your customers then you know this: one of them owns his own bus.

I don't drive it. I don't have a license. However the fact that I own it is fascinating enough.

You may be wondering why I own a bus but I don't have a license. Well my friends, that's a secret I plan to keep. For now.

However, if you have any Shell freebies, such as a tee shirt or suchlike, I might write back with the story of how I came to own my own bus. Then, you would have all the facts at your disposal.

Thanks for your interest,

James Spence

Shell U.K. Oil Products Limited
Retail Customer Service
Rowlandsway House
Rowlandsway
Wythenshawe
Manchester
M22 5SB
Tel 0800 731 8888
Fax 0161 933 3227
Internet http://www.shell.com/uk

7th May 2008

Dear Mr Spence,

Thank you for your email dated 6th May 2008.

Please find enclosed a Ferrari Model Car and a sheet of Shell emblem stickers.

I am very entrigued to hear the rest of your story and wish you every success with your bus.

Thank you for contacting Shell UK.

Regards

Paul Smith
Customer Service Professional

FERRARI AND STICKERS

To: Tetley
From: James Spence
Subject: Tea's Company

I wrote a poem in tribute to your wonderful tea:

Tetley are the people who enrich my life each day,
I need my morning cuppa, to take my blues away.
I sipped it in the eighties, (back when I had a mullet)
I drank it in the nineties (and poured it down my gullet)
I gulp it in the noughties with cunning and with guile
I think I'll always love it 'cause it always makes me smile

Do you have a (large) Tetley T-shirt for a loyal fan?
Cheers,

James Spence

To: James Spence
From: Tetley
Subject: Re: Tea's Company

Dear James

I am sorry to say that we have no T-Shirts available, however I will pop some goodies in the post to you as your poem brightened up our day!

Kind regards

Lizzi Chambers

Tetley GB Consumer Services

To:	Converse
From:	James Spence
Subject:	The Con Man

Good Morrow Makers of Fine Sneakers,

I have a well-crafted pair of red Converse All Stars, as well made as the hammer of Odin himself. These sturdy Converse foot-cloths are more comfortable than the skin of a buck and more importantly, make me look 'cool'. Many is the day when I strut around in my Cons and turn heads from every direction. I suppose the other reason I turn heads could be that I am, in fact, a Viking from days of old transported into the future by a 'Time Spank'.

The future is indeed a strange place with many surprises around every corner. I've had to dramatically alter the way I live my life. Unfortunately for me, longboats are very tough to come by these days, so instead I roam from town to town looting and plundering in a blue Triumph Herald (it was the closest thing I could find). I do however have to keep getting it re-upholstered as the long horns on my helmet keep tearing the material inside. I guess I could just remove my helmet. Damn. I wish I'd thought of that earlier.

Anyway, it's a tough life being a Viking in this day and age, but with my red Cons, I am capable of sneaking up to many of my victims and capturing them without a fuss. Most of my prisoners have commented on how nice my sneakers are, and that's all down to you fine people. I thank you.

As a busy Viking, I have little time to master the customs of the modern age (although as you are reading this email, you can see I have mastered the Internet). I yearn to become a more modern viking and blend into this strange new society. The only way I can think of to do this is to get myself a tee shirt. I will then look just like everyone else (except of course for my five-foot beard, Viking helmet and sledgehammer).

I therefore wondered if you, the makers of my red Cons had any Converse tee shirts (large or extra large) lying about. I would wear it with pride, and would avoid getting it messed up in my raids. Unfortunately, I have no money, as a Viking from the past and so this would have to be a gift from you to me. I would thank you from the bottom of my belly.

May courage fuel your kipper,

James Longhorn Spence

To: Flymo
From: James Spence
Subject: A Cut Above

Dear Flymo,

I write to tell you of a strange event that happened to me thanks to one of your expertly crafted lawnmowers.

It was a winter morning and I had awoken early. I got out of bed in darkness to avoid waking my wife from her well-earned rest.

In the shadowy atmosphere of the house, I felt my way towards the kitchen to make a packed lunch. Is food worth eating if it's not out of a plastic container?

With arms outstretched I placed my hands on the fridge and opened the door. The fridge light illuminated the kitchen in a welcoming glow as I identified the necessary ingredients: bread, butter, jam, whelks, pickled camel gums and a fresh chuckberry. I also picked up the items I wanted to eat that night for my dinner: salmon tarts, three turkey snouts and a bear's egg.

I closed the fridge door, turned around and much to my surprise, tripped over a very unexpected Flymo. My lunch ingredients flew up into the air, and I swiftly flipped over the Flymo in order to catch them on it's underside.

In the confusion, I switched the blasted thing on, firing the sliced up foodstuff in every direction: up, down, left, right, back and up again.

At first, I was furious, suspecting that the food was wasted. It was, proving my first instinct correct.

However, when my eyes adjusted I smelt something unexpected. I had somehow invented the flavour of 'remorse'. I regretted it, of course, especially as my favourite tee shirt (it emitted weasel sounds) was covered in the weird-feeling stuff.

I write therefore to congratulate you on the effectiveness of your wonderful product. Many of you rivals out there probably couldn't cut a lawn let alone invent a new flavour! I also write because I wondered if you had a (large) Flymo tee shirt to replace the one I lost to the taste of remorse.

Many thanks, and keep up the good work,

James Spence

To: Wedgewood
From: James Spence
Subject: Dishy

Hi there,

I really admire your company and wanted to drop you an email to show my appreciation for your work. At the moment, I am enjoying a fine mug of tea (filled to the brim) from a very well crafted mug. You make a very impressive set of crockery. My good friend and house guest Dr Sebastian did not buy me anything when I got married but had he bought me Wedgewood I would have been very happy. My wife (Tiffany) and I love your dishes. I do however have a sad story to tell...

A month or so back, I found myself watching a rented DVD and enjoying pizza off a plate. Disaster struck! The topping-heavy pizza slice dropped onto my favourite tee shirt (it had an owl on it - the tee shirt, not the pizza), ruining it. A few days later and as I drank from my wonderful mug whilst practising my unicycle act, I took the mug away from my lips a little too early dribbling tea onto my second favourite tee shirt (depicting a mermaid on stilts). A couple of months back, whilst drinking soup from a bowl during a brief stint with a pneumatic drill, I dropped onions onto my A-team tee shirt. A few days later and while pogo-sticking through the house with a bowl of spaghetti, some of it splashed onto my Mystery Frog of Doom tee shirt, devaluing it completely!

I can't figure out why I keep dropping food onto my shirts. It may be down to my good friend and house guest Dr Sebastian, who enjoys a game of 'trip the food carrier' whenever he can. However, as he has diplomatic immunity I'd be a fool to try and seek recompense from him! Perhaps it is the fault of my cat, who jumps on my head while I eat? Maybe it is my lovely wife's fault. She calls me a 'clumsy oaf' and throws sprouts at me after the spillages happen, so perhaps she causes them somehow? I can't work it out!

The one thing I do know however, is that NONE of this is the fault of Wedgewood, whose superb crockery had never smashed, chipped or melted during my antics. I do have a hole in my tee shirt collection, but it's not your fault! However, as an admirer of your company, I did wonder if you, the mighty and beautiful Wedgewood had a large tee shirt for a huge fan.

If wearing it whilst eating, I'll wear a bib.

Well done on some great crockery,

James Spence

To: James Spence
From: Wedgewood
Subject: Re: Dishy

Hi James,

Thanks for the kind comments concerning our company.

What a sad story - I think all Fifers are clumsy (I'm married to one).

For your cheek I will send you a very special shirt but you must only wear it when you are not eating, drinking, watching telly, riding your bike, running a marathon or climbing Mount Everest. I've chosen a special colour for you, make sure you treat it with extreme care!!!

Eileen

To: Whirlpool
From: James Spence
Subject: Washed Out

Greetings Washing Machine Masters,

The other day, I found myself standing in a subway waiting for a train with my Whirlpool washing machine strapped to my back. After what seemed like a century, the train finally arrived.

Yes, I was nervous as that night would be my debut performance of "Me and my Washing Machine", a stage show I'd wanted to participate in since I first heard about it during my nude cycling tour of Europe. Fate intervened and I was successful in my audition, having been picked from a thousand potential candidates due to my washing machine juggling abilities and strong arms and spleen.

As I took my seat in the train, I noticed some girls were watching me and my Whirlpool, so I did my special 'hunk' face. They must have liked it because they said I was some character and wondered if they could have their photo taken with the machine. I swiftly identified the girl I liked best and threw the washing machine at her, breaking her spindly arms in one fell swoop. Sensing that I had outstayed my welcome at this point, I ran for it.

These events happened on Sunday, and so far the police have not been in touch, which is weird because in the confusion I took one of the girl's arms with me.

Anyway, you're probably wondering why I'm telling you this. The reason, saviours, is that I need a disguise so I don't get rumbled, and the only disguise I can think of is a new tee shirt.

Can you send me a (large) Whirlpool tee shirt? That would really save my neck! Many thanks and well done on a great range of washing machines,

James Spence

To: Cambridge Dictionary
From: James Spence
Subject: Shirty Questions

Salutations Word Masters,

I write to you because I'm something of a tee shirt nut, and I have a word problem!

I used the Cambridge English Dictionary web site to look up 'tee shirt' and discovered that both 'tee shirt' and 't shirt' were acceptable ways of writing my favourite garment. However, this causes me a problem. You see I'm writing a book on the aforementioned shirts and I'm not sure which spelling is the better of the two. Both have their own merits:

Tee shirt is a little longer, therefore would 'pad' out my book more, deceiving the customer into believing they were getting more for their money. In addition, I think it looks more aesthetically pleasing. It is also more likely to interest golfing fanatics as the word 'tee' sends them into euphoria.

T shirt is shorter and would allow me to write my book faster. It is less wearing on the 'e' key on my keyboard. It would allow people to read my book faster, and therefore would appeal to busy executives, housewives and racing drivers.

If you could let me know which of these is better I'd be most grateful. Is there anything wrong with using both? What about tea shirt? Who invented the tee shirt?

Do you have a (large) Cambridge English Dictionary (or similar) tee shirt for a loyal customer and fan?

Thank you a million times and thanks for a great Dictionary,

James Spence

To: James Spence
From: Cambridge Dictionary
Subject: Re: Shirty Questions

Dear James,

Thanks for your message. Though all are permitted variants, I believe T-shirt is the standard spelling for this word. So, it's fewer key strokes and a lowered risk of RSI!

All the best with your book.

Kate Woodford

To:	Dyson
From:	James Spence
Subject:	You Suck (In a Good Way)

Good Day Suction Experts,

I write to tell you of a strange tale that directly relates to your company. Read on, my friends, please read on...

My mum (Astrid) has recently purchased one of your Dyson cleaners and simply cannot believe how fantastic it is. She's been trying to persuade me to 'bite the bullet' and get one of these puppies too. I must confess, at first, I was not convinced by her mere words, but after she went on and on about it, I reluctantly agreed to borrow her beloved Dyson (which we've named Harold) to try it out.

I must say I was very impressed with the results. The carpets look as though they are brand new and the house no longer smells of tuna (following a fish-related mishap last month). The joy was short lived, however. You see, I'm a 'thinking outside the box' kind of fellow and having seen the impressive results on the carpet, I had an unusual idea...

Several weeks ago, whilst watching a comedy DVD I had rented, I accidentally dropped pizza onto my favourite shirt (it had an owl on it), rendering it permanently stained. I had tried washing it several times, but the sauce just would not come out. At the time it drove me crazy!

So it should come as no surprise that I had a flash of inspiration. I had tried washing the stain, and I had tried rubbing the stain, but I hadn't tried Dysoning the stain (with Harold the Dyson).

I carefully spread the shirt out on the floor, stain-side up and powered up the Dyson. I admit, it was a long shot and at the back of my mind I knew there was a chance it wouldn't work. To my amazement however, the Dyson seemed to suck the stain out of the shirt!!! I could not believe my eyes!! My favourite shirt was restored to its former glory, and I had an owl tee shirt again.

Miracles really do happen, my friends.

You may well think that this story has a happy ending, but alas no. For when I put on my favourite owl tee shirt, I tripped over the Dyson and in my frantic fall, ripped the aforementioned shirt on my cactus plant (we named him Barney).

Now, I know this isn't Dyson's fault. Heck, Dyson are the heroes of this tale. If anything, I should take this out on Barney and his relentlessly spiky ways. However, I just can't stay mad at him.

Therefore, I've elected to chalk this one up to experience. No more cleaning the house in moon boots for me.

At the end of this strange and unusual tale I'm left one tee shirt down. I therefore find myself writing to ask if you, the Dyson heroes of the hour, have any (large) Dyson tee shirts knocking about? If so, It'll take pride of place in my wardrobe (Jeremy).

Thanks a bunch, Dyson. You are fantastic.

James Spence

To: Stella Artois
From: James Spence
Subject: New Beer

Dear Stella Artois,

I write to thank you from the bottom of my heart for Stella Artois. After a hard day rummaging for ingredients for my experimental foods out in the woods, I like nothing better than to come home, put up my feet and settle down with a good bottle of Stella Artois (or twenty!).

I write to tell of a sorry incident that happened to me following a glass or two of your fine beer. I had just finished inventing a device called 'The jaminator' for dispensing jam onto bread evenly, when a thought struck me! Wouldn't it be terrific if there was a flavoured beer that tasted of jam or indeed other foods?

Please don't dismiss this one off hand, for I immediately turned to my 'mixinator' (a device I came up with several years back for mixing ingredients together). I poured in a full bottle of Stella and two scoops of gooseberry jam and clicked the mixinator to mixinate mode seven and waited while it powered.

The gloopy substance that came out of the mixinator's hose was most unusual. It was a little sickly and unpleasant, but overall not horrible.

The next experiment was sprout Stella. The 'sproutinator' (a device I came up with on holiday for selecting sprouts) put several sprouts into the mixinator. The resulting substance was revolting and gave me the tummy wibbles.

When I then operated the 'prune-juiceinator' (a device for painting walls, that doubles as a storage space for prune juice), I subsequently poured Stella into the mixinator. The resulting substance was delicious.

You may think this story has a happy ending. Prune juice beer will probably sell like hot-cakes (I'm working on a hot-cakeinator), but alas the story does not end in smiles yet. Sadly, the mixinator does not have a lid and while making these delightful brews, my favourite tee shirt (it depicts squirrel racing) was destroyed. I cried.

Then out of the blue, I had a great idea! What if you wonderful people had a (large) Stella Artois tee shirt you could send to a loyal customer?

Keep up the brilliant work, Stella. Feel free to use my prune beer idea free of charge!

Thanks,

James Spence

To: BT Yahoo
From: James Spence
Subject: World Wise Web

Hi there,

This isn't actually a complaint, but you didn't have a box to tick for 'compliment'. I wanted to write and say how fantastic a job you guys do. I get speedy results every time I access the web. Well done chaps!

Here's a brief poem in tribute to the work you do:

I like to use the Internet. It's the high point in my life.

It's how I do my shopping. It's how I met my wife.

I like to go online for movies, songs and chat.

Thanks to BT Yahoo broadband, I can do all that!

You may wish to use that in a staff newsletter or advertising campaign? I would love a (large) BT Yahoo tee shirt, if such a thing exists.

Thanks very, very much,

James Spence

Yahoo Complaints Team.

BT openworld

With compliments

Val xxx, Katie xx, Kati xx, Gary, Surinder xx, Rihana xx, Tracy x, Roy, David, Sharon xx, Vikki xx, Tas xx, Matt, Barry, Margaret xx, Ambreen xx, Russell, Simon, Amanda xx, Xavier + Chris, Brian. Ben. Paul,

www.btopenworld.com

Poem and Tee Shirt

BT

Thank you for your comments; they are very nice indeed,
It is the type of email that we really like to receive,
You asked us for a T-Shirt, and we've found one lying round,
It hasn't been used by anyone, and isn't off the ground,
We hope that when you're wearing it you will find it will suit you,
Please take it with our compliments from all at BT Yahoo!

To:	Princes
From:	James Spence
Subject:	A Tuna Day

Hi there Tuna Providers,

I am a chap who loves tuna. Tuna is the greatest fish the world has ever seen. Better than cod by a long shot. And mackerel? Don't make me laugh!! I've never met a tuna in the wild, but I dare say if I did, I'd like to shake him by the hand (paw?)

I digress.

This email has been sent to you because I needed to get something off my chest. Yes, I am a tuna fan, but I'm afraid I have a tragic 'Princes Tuna' story to tell...

I live with my friend Sebastian (a doctor), normally a decent sort. He and I were watching a particularly good episode of Doctor Who (it was an Ice Warrior story) when suddenly hunger struck. I asked Sebastian if he was hungry but he didn't answer, so engrossed was he in the episode - he's a Who nut!

I got up and headed for the fridge to see what I could get to quash those hunger pains. The fridge was largely empty: a few cans of lager, some eggs, prunes, chilli sauce and punnet of lard. However, right at the back, under my journals, was a can of Princes tuna I had not even realised I owned!

Thinking my luck was in, I promptly made (and largely consumed) a tuna sandwich, enjoying every last chunk (morsel?) of your fine fishy goodness. I then returned to Sebastian and our Doctor Who marathon with a half-eaten tuna sandwich. This is where the story goes downhill...

Sebastian didn't so much as speak to me upon my return. It transpired that the tuna I had enjoyed so vivaciously was his and it was not my place to devour it so greedily. The fight that ensued was not one that I will discuss in detail but, needless to say, it was pretty wild and my favourite tee shirt (it had a picture of a potato on it) was destroyed by fire. The remainder of the tuna sandwich was smeared into our cactus.

Sebastian has not spoken to me since and I still don't know if the Doctor saved the world from the Ice Warriors, as Sebastian has hidden the DVD.

You see, delicious tuna is a good thing, but not worth losing a good friend and tee shirt over.

I realise that there is nothing you can do to restore my friendship with Sebastian, but I wondered if you happened to have a spare Princes' tee shirt lying around to replace the shirt I lost in the incident described above.

Thanks so much for the fantastic tuna. I enjoy it every day on my sandwich at work. You guys do a brilliant job.

Well done all of you,

James Spence

To: Aquafresh
From: James Spence
Subject: Minted

Hi Grin-makers,

Thanks chaps, for granting me the greatest grin in all the land! That's right! I'm 28 and don't have a single filling. Not one! It's all thanks to two brushings a day with Aquafresh.

I thought I'd write for three reasons: 1, I wanted to thank you for helping me stay filling-free! 2, I had a few product ideas you may want to try out and c, I wanted to ask for an Aquafresh tee shirt (like I say, I'm a big fan!)

1. Thank You
2. A few product ideas: Aquafresh is a great toothpaste, but sometimes I grow weary of mint and yearn for a different taste before bedtime. Have you considered the merits of some of these flavours: Strawberry, cherry, apricot, milk, cornflakes, beef, corn-on-the-cob, soup, bubblegum or cream of duck?
3. I am a massive fan of Aquafresh. Please may I have a large Aquafresh t-shirt?

Thanks,

James Spence

To: James Spence
From: Aquafresh
Subject: Re: Minted

Thank you for your recent email message. We were delighted to hear of the good results you have had by using our Aquafresh Toothpaste. Although we have the utmost confidence in our products, it is always rewarding to hear from a satisfied customer. Please be assured that your comments will be passed to our Marketing Department for reference.

You may not be aware that we have 3 new flavours in the Aquafresh range - Refresh Zones - Mint fused with Apple refreshment, Mint fused with Watermelon quench and Mint fused with Lemon invigoration.

We have noted the contents of your email messages and have highlighted your comments to our Marketing Department for their information. As we are continually assessing our products with regard to packaging etc., we are grateful that you have gone to the trouble of letting us know your views.

We have today put a sample of the new flavours in the post to you for you to try out at your own convenience.

Once again thank you for taking the time to contact us.

Kind regards,

Consumer Affairs Department

GLAXOSMITHKLINE CONSUMER HEALTHCARE

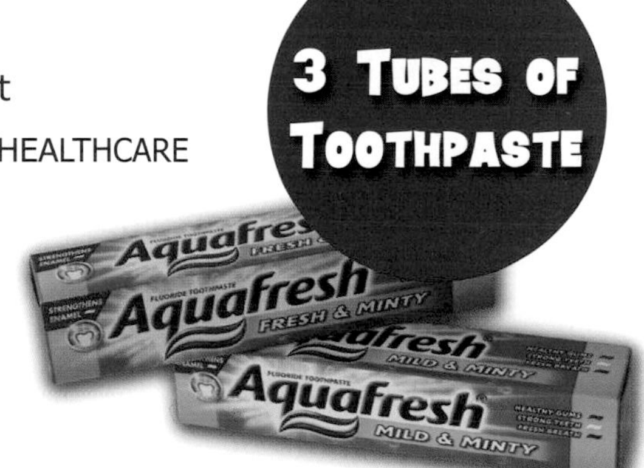

To:	Fruit of the Loom
From:	James Spence
Subject:	Fruity

Hi there,

I wanted to write to congratulate you on your underpants!!
I absolutely love wearing Fruit of the Loom underwear. It is by far the most comfortable underwear money can buy (or perhaps rent?).

Several years back, I was attacked by a guard-wombat whilst attempting to steal valuables from my best friend's house. I soon healed, but my pride was injured, and I turned to the fridge for comfort. As the years passed, I ballooned up to a whopping 730 pounds and had to be lowered into my bed each night using a pulley system engineered by my local boy scout troop.

All this changed, however, when I met Tiffany (she'd come to one of my magic shows) and we fell in love. She persuaded me that if I lost weight, we could be wed, and I went into overdrive, slimming right down to a slender 70 pounds. This did not please her and she threatened to dump me if I did not gain some weight. She felt that if I looked like a living skeleton, it would make her look fat in the wedding pictures. I stopped going to the gym and again hit the fridge. Before long I had piled on the pounds again, back up to a respectable 170 pounds.

My only problem now is that all my clothes are either too big to wear (but fine to camp in) or too small to wear (but fine for dressing up my cat, Angel, and taking amusing pictures).

Due to the amount I have had to pay in gym fees, food, weight loss products, weight gain products, lard, fitness equipment and pumps, I have no money left for buying clothes, and am having to wash my one outfit (a tee shirt and pair of underpants) every third night.

I therefore write to ask if you, the mighty corporation 'Fruit of the Loom', would open your heart and send a former fat/thin guy a voucher for clothing, or better yet, a (large) Fruit of the Loom tee shirt (and/or replacement pair of underpants)?

I promise to keep my weight at this level. From now on I'll only eat Fruit (possibly from the Loom!!)

Keep up the good work wonder-dudes. Thanks for all your great work.

James Spence

To: Panini
From: James Spence
Subject: The Sticky Stuff

Hi there Panini Heroes,

I'm a huge fan of Panini. I think that you are the best
When it comes to comics and stickers,
you're simply ahead of the rest.

For years I have purchased your products.
I've admired your top quality,
There's nothing as great as your company.
That's why I love Panini.

I'd love a Panini tee shirt. It would be a fabulous thing
I'd wear it each day and be happy.
Think of the joy you would bring!

Well done on being fantastic. I'm really a very big fan,
So how about granting that tee shirt?
I'd be an ecstatic young man!

Thanks,

James Spence

To:	James Spence
From:	Panini
Subject:	Re: The Sticky Stuff

Hi James

Thank you for your recent e-mail to Panini.

I'm really sorry but we don't have any Panini t-shirts, but for such a great effort with your rhyme I'll be more than happy to send you some stickers.

Let me know which collections take your interest and I'll see what I can sort out for you.

I look forward to hearing from you.

Kind Regards

Becky Lee

To: Washburn Guitars
From: James Spence
Subject: Guitar Gods

Greetings Guitar Gods,

Let us take a trip back in time to Christmas 1990. I was awoken by the sound of reindeer hooves clattering against my ceiling and quickly donned my ceremonial Christmas head monkey and raced downstairs to see what Father Christmas had brought me.

To my amazement instead of the usual pile of hubcaps and aerials that Santa had got his thieving hands on, there was a brand spanking new Washburn Electric Guitar (later named "Loretta" after the Doctor who bungled my implants).

Loretta and I spend many happy hours together. I practiced and jammed and honed my skills, developing the ability to 'rock out' without much advance notice. I soon learned some tricks, such as playing with my feet, eyes or hands. My status as Rock Legend was assured until, one day in the mid nineties tragedy struck.

I lost my taste in music.

It started innocently enough with a foot tap to catchy Vanilla Ice tune, but went downhill from there. Spears, O'Donnell, Streisand, Twain and Midler all entered my life. Westlife, Boyzone, All Saints, Backstreet Boys and NSync followed. It was a disaster. Friends shunned me. Strangers pointed and laughed. Even the deaf hated me for abusing the gift of sound.

It looked as though all hope was lost. Then, just as I was about to take the final step towards total taste annihilation (i.e. buying a Celine Dion album), my Washburn guitar stepped in and saved my soul.

Read on my friends...

Loretta had followed me into my local music shop. From afar, she watched as I reached out my small furry hand and touched the Dion disc, then with no thought for her own personal safety, leapt between me and the album. Yes, Loretta took the hit for me.

Immediately I came to my senses and realised the error of my ways. Zeppelin, Purple, the Doors, the Who, the Stones energised me and returned my Rock Legend status. My taste impediment had vanished, and it was all thanks to the Washburn.

I owe you my eardrums dudes. Any chance of a Washburn tee shirt? That would freakin' rock, dudes!!

Boomshanka!!!!

James Spence

To: James Spence
From: Washburn Guitars
Subject: Re: Guitar Gods

Thank you, that was the greatest "free t-shirt" e-mail we have ever received. What size do you wear?

Mike Beatty

Customer Service Manager

To:	The Economist
From:	James Spence
Subject:	It All Adds Up

Dear the Economist,

I've been a practising Economist for several years and was delighted to discover that there was a journal devoted to my favourite pastime! It is heart-warming to know that there are others out there still enjoying the art of stuffing wild cats, foxes, otters and perhaps even bears.

I learned how to be an economist from my grandfather who once even stuffed a rhino and mounted it in his bedroom, beneath the head of a wild elk.

When I first started studying economy, I began as so many of us do, stuffing whatever birds I could find. I recall with great fondness the first time I got my hands on a tit. Ah sweet memories.

The other week, as I was extracting the entrails of a Clydesdale (good eatin' that night!), I looked down and noticed that my favourite economist tee shirt (it had a picture of a stuffed monkey on it) had got covered in horse-goop! A thought then struck me! What if the Economist made promotional tee shirts? Would I be deserving of such an item? Please let me know. I eagerly await a reply.

Keep up the good work. I have not yet read your journal, but plan to flick through it tonight whilst sewing up a beaver. Perhaps there will be a few tips in the mag?

Well done on keeping the art alive and please let me know about the tee!

James Spence

To: Ben & Jerry's
From: James Spence
Subject: Freeze a Jolly Good Fella

Hello there Ice Cream Hero's!

I can't believe I'm actually emailing THE Ben and Jerry's company. You are THE BEST. I just had to write and tell you guys how fabbo you are. I ADORE your ice cream goodness. I eat it, like, ALL the time. Have you considered trying new flavours like marmalade, chocolate lemon or egg. I even wrote this poem about your company:

Ben and Jerry's Ice Cream is really rather good.
It's better than the other brands (but I don't mean to be rude)
It's fun and it's delicious with flavours that I like,
If I didn't have it, I'd get on my bike...
And cycle to my local shop, by going o'er the bridge,
Once I got there I would run, and jump into the fridge!
The shopkeeper'd get angry. He'd run and shake his fist!
But my love of Ben and Jerry's isn't easily dismissed!

I LOVE Ben and Jerry's ice cream. Do you have a (large) t-shirt for a loyal and enthusiastic fan? I tell everyone about Ben and Jerry's.

Thanks a million for everything you do. You must be really proud to work at Ben and Jerry's.

Thanks,

James Spence

To: James Spence
From: Ben & Jerry's
Subject: Re: Freeze a Jolly Good Fella

Hi James,

Thanks for your e-mail from which I was pleased to learn that you are such a fan of Ben & Jerry's ice cream.

I loved your poem and have popped a t-shirt in the post to you for your efforts!

Hope you continue to be a fan for many years to come.

Lisa Dale

Ben & Jerry's UK

To:	Hooters
From:	James Spence
Subject:	Awooga!

Greetings Hooters Heroines,

I've just returned home to Scotland from sunny Florida on vacation. I had a fabulous time, and it was largely due to my visit to "Hooters". The very concept of great food, friendly staff and skimpy outfits is pure genius and I applaud you. I am saving as we speak to come back to the USA and enjoy many more fantastic Hooters meals.

I had a truly wonderful time during my visit. The waitresses were exceptionally friendly and attentive. I'm normally a very fussy eater but somehow I managed to consume the meal without giving it a second thought, as though I were somehow distracted. I just remember it must have been particularly delicious as I recall salivating profusely.

The only factor limiting my full enjoyment of the meal was the repeated 'smacks' around the head I experienced each time my eyes strayed from my wife's beautiful face. During these 'playful' beatings, much of the delicious meal found it's way down my tee shirt, and I think I suffered a mild concussion, although my memory has been somewhat sketchy since the visit.

I do however recall at one point my eyes strayed towards our waitress's cleavage as she took our order. My wife's loving head-butt soon corrected that error, and the matter was rapidly forgotten. Except, of course, by her. The doctors informed me that the cricket bat blow to my cranium has resulted on only minor brain damage and I'll be able speak without slurring within the next two years.

At the end of our meal, I left a generous tip for the waitress. Of course, the true cost of that was the temporary loss of my vision due to the unexpected chair that crashed against the back of my head. Nevertheless, I feel that the tip was well earned.

I did have one suggestion, however, for your gift shop. I for one would love to see a Hooters first aid kit, complete with painkillers and head bandages. I know I'd have found a use for it!

Yes, my Hooters experience was truly wonderful, although I did unfortunately ruin my favourite tee shirt during the meal. I wondered if you could send me a (large) Hooters tee shirt to replace the one that was destroyed during my visit.

Many thanks and well done on a great restaurant! Hoot on my friends, hoot on,

James Spence

To: Penguin Books
From: James Spence
Subject: Penguin Questions

Hi there,

I'm full of admiration for Penguin Books, but must admit I have several questions!

- How do you hold the books if all you have are flippers?
- What is your monthly fish bill?
- Are all things at your company black and white issues?
- If you eat Penguin biscuits, is that cannibalism?

Anyway, I just wanted to ask these important questions and also tell you how great I think your company is. Any chance of a (large) penguin t-shirt?

Thanks and give my compliments to the Emperor,

James Spence

To: James Spence
From: Penguin Books
Subject: Re: Penguin Questions

Hi there,

Here are some answers for your questions as requested:

- We hold our books with our feet.
- Our bills are a lot as there are a lot of penguins in the company
- We do some coloured books.
- Some might say it is cannibalism but we would say other wise.

Unfortunately we do not supply t shirts, but thanks for the email.

Sara Bacon

UK Customer Services

To:	JJB Sports
From:	James Spence
Subject:	Sporty, Sporty

Dear JJB Sports,

Happy New Year!

An idea hit me recently, and I feel duty bound to share it with the world at large, and you, the good people at JJB, can be the medium of this message. I think we're having a moment here!

You see I recently realised that if my car had bigger wheels, then each time they (the wheels) turned a full rotation, my car would move a greater distance. If you don't believe it, try it out with biscuits: A full rotation of a Rich Tea will go further than a full rotation of a Jaffa Cake. Therefore, the bigger my wheels are, the further I travel on the same amount of petrol.

However, as my car is very small, there is only a limited amount of space under the wheel arches. This fact alone would make many a lesser man give up, and shake his fist at God, screaming 'Why do you mock me, grand poombah? Did I not offer up the right sacrifices?'

Not I.

I have the solution. Oh yes. If I were to glue cricket bats around each wheel then my wheels will effectively become larger (see picture) and my petrol bill smaller.

However, I do not have twenty-four cricket bats, and probably never will have. But you probably do!! So for the good of humanity I pass this idea on to you to take into development and then on to the general public at large. Lucky bastards.

All I ask in return is a (large) JJB tee shirt, or if you don't have such a thing, a JJB pen or other item of JJB merchandise would do nicely. Even an old item from your staff canteen (i.e. lumpy milk?) would thrill me to my very socks.

Keep up the great work. I love shopping at JJB for all my sport accessory needs.

Anyone for cricket?,

James Spence

To: James Spence
From: JJB Sports
Subject: Re: Sporty, Sporty

Dear Mr Spence,

You have obviously offered up the right sacrifices but since we are out of both Rich Tea and Jaffa Cakes I can't manage to get you a cricket bat. I am however sending you a large JJB t-shirt under separate cover which you can wear to your cricket matches. If you ever achieve a patent on your cricket bat wheels let me know.

In the meantime thank you for your continued support.

Lena Maguire

PA to the Chairman & Chief Executive

To: Matalan
From: James Spence
Subject: Model Citizen

Dear Matalan,

It is my dream to become a model. Please read on, for the image of Matalan may be about to change forever.

I think I could be the new 'face' of Matalan in your future advertising campaigns, and so I write to offer my services. While not a celebrity (yet!), I do wander around a lot and therefore have quite a high profile in my local town of Dunfermline. This is enhanced because I stop people in the street a lot to ask for spare change.

My face is also very unique on account of my enormous nose, ears and throat. I have several interesting facial imperfections that are sure to draw in attention, such as my extra nostril, beak and antenna. I am also bald, cross-eyed and as a result of a foolish bet, have the word 'grief' tattooed on my forehead.

Unfortunately, I don't have any photos as, for some reason, my image can't be captured on film. I realise that this may set back my plans to become a model, as my image will have to be sketched afterwards in by a skilled artist.

Please let me know if my services will be required. If not, please could you send me a (large) Matalan tee shirt so that I can pretend to live the dream at home, parading up and down my hall.

Yours, with fingers crossed I get a Matalan tee shirt. I love shopping at Matalan,

James Spence

To:	Slim Fast
From:	James Spence
Subject:	Heavy Weight

Hi there,

Just wanted to write to say how terrific Slim Fast is. It is my first week trying out the 'Slim Fast' scheme and I can't wait to weigh myself at the end of the week and find out how much I've lost. You truly are the geniuses who invented thinness in a can!

It has been an easy week so far! I drank two Slim Fast shakes a day as per the rules, plus have gorged myself on cakes, wine, chocolate bars and my favourite (jellied trotters with snouts in fish dribblings). Mmm. Makes the mouth water just thinking about it. I don't know how the Slim Fast process works (I guess somehow the shake 'eats' the food inside my belly). However it works, I like it!!

I wondered if you could send me a Slim Fast tee shirt so I could proudly display my new slim-line bod and endorse your company. XXL if you have one, if not, a XL or L will do nicely.

Many thanks and well done on a great diet! Those tasty shakes are too good to be true!!

Shake it up a notch,

James Spence

Slim-Fast Consumer Care
Freepost NATE139
Milton Keynes
MK9 1BR

Phone: 0845 600 1311
Minicom: 0800 0280173
E-mail: consumer@slimfast.co.uk
Website: www.slimfast.co.uk

Ref: 470349
Date: 19 January 2005

Mr J Spence 470349

Dear Mr Spence

Thank you for contacting Slim•Fast.

The Plan is designed for your convenience and tailored for your individual lifestyle. You should replace two meals a day with your chosen meal replacements and your third meal of the day should be a healthy, nutritious meal of 600 calories for women and 800 for men.

In addition to your three meals you should have three daily snacks and each snack should be 100 calories. We do recommend having fruit for snacks.

Ready cooked meals are allowed provided that you choose the low fat healthy option meals. You should check the calorie content on the packaging and if it falls below the calorie limit you should make up the balance with extra vegetables or salad items.

In addition, we do recommend that you increase your fluid intake to 3-4 pints per day. Tea and coffee are allowed using skimmed milk and replacing sugar with sweetener. Water is, of course, fine and canned drinks are allowed provided they are the diet or low calorie variety.

Research shows that people who include physical activity in their weight loss programme are more likely to keep the weight off than people who only change their diet. Exercise will also help you to feel and look better.

It is important that exercise does not have to be strenuous or lengthy to be beneficial. Walking is acknowledged by experts to be one of the most effective exercises and almost anyone can do it! Begin with a 15-20 minute walk three times a week and build your stamina until you can walk briskly for 30 minutes at least three times a week.

Swimming, cycling and dancing are also great forms of exercise. Pick an activity that you enjoy. Remember that any increase in activity will help. We recommend that you check with your doctor before starting any type of exercise programme.

We recommend that any consumers wishing to commence the Plan who may be on a form of long-term medication should always consult their doctor in case their medication may need a slight adjustment.

If you have access to the Internet, please log on to our website, www.slimfast.co.uk for recipe ideas, the online club and further advice and support.

If you would like any further information or advice please call the Careline number 0845 600 1311, Monday to Friday from 8.45am to 5pm, or contact us via e-mail at consumers@slimfast.co.uk, and one of our advisors will be happy to help you.

Yours sincerely

Rosetta Pozzuto
Consumer Care Advisor

--
Enclosures:
1 x Slim•Fast Leaflet
1 x Slim•Fast Calorie Counter Booklet
1 x Slim•Fast Diary
1 x Slim•Fast Product List
2 x Slim•Fast Recipes
1 x Slim•Fast Snacking Leaflet
1 x Slim•Fast T-Shirt

INFORMATION PACK AND TEE SHIRT

To: Guinness
From: James Spence
Subject: The Black Stuff

Hi there Makers of Guinness,

Thank you so much for Guinness. As a mass consumer, I wanted to write and tell you chaps how smashing I think you and your product are.

I have a few suggestions for other products you may wish to sell:

- Guinness pies. You heard me! My wife makes 'Steak and Guinness Pies'. (Email for recipe!) They're delicious. What I was thinking was 'wouldn't it be skill if Guinness sold the pies ready made. I could 'nuke' one when returning from the pub.
- Guinness jam. For breakfast consumption. I like a Guinness with my toast in the morning. Sometimes, I have been known to 'dunk' the toast in the Guinness, thereby enhancing the toasty goodness. One day, it struck me! If Guinness made jam, I could have Guinness on my toast without having to endure the strange glances of my wife (Tiffany) and others.
- Guinness 'keg-hats' - (not for people with brittle necks)

Can I have a large tee shirt?

Thanks,

James Spence

To: Andrex
From: James Spence
Subject: Get Into the Groove

Hi there Puppy Producers!

I am a customer of yours and Sebastian is a HUGE fan of the Andrex puppy. Although Sebastian isn't much of a talker, you can tell that he takes great delight in the Andrex puppy. Several years ago we saved tokens and got a stuffed puppy (How many puppies died in that promo?! Just kidding!) which Sebastian is rarely seen without. So I wrote a poem, for Sebastian's sake:

Sebastian, Sebastian - Perhaps your biggest fan?
To see him with his puppy, makes me a happy man.
Sebastian's not the smartest - he'll never be a yuppy!
He thinks the Andrex company manufactures puppies!
I try to tell him otherwise but he doesn't understand.
Despite it all Sebastian is... still your biggest fan.

I wondered if you had an Andrex tee shirt (preferably with the puppy on it) for Sebastian. He'd be cock-a-hoop! I'd send a photo of him in it.

Thanks Andrex,

James Spence

 Kimberly-Clark

20 August 2004

Mr. James Spence

Dear Mr. Spence,

Thank you for your recent e-mail regarding ANDREX® Puppy Collection.

We are always pleased to receive comments from consumers, especially when they are so complimentary.

Unfortunately we do not have an Andrex t-shirt, I enclose the offers available at present.

Thank you for taking the time to contact us and please find enclosed, with our compliments, a goodwill gesture.

Yours sincerely,

Emilie Wilson
Consumer Services D

00115519

To: British Potato Council
From: James Spence
Subject: A Chip on My Shoulder

Greetings spud enthusiasts,

It's great to contact fellow potato lovers. I am a huge fan of potato. I love them and have dedicated hours of my free time painstakingly researching and analysing potato facts. These facts I now donate to you free of charge for your literature.

A Brief History of the Potato

The name POTATO is an acronym for Plant Offering Tastiness and Always Tantalisingly Obscene. It was invented in 1945 by Johnny 'Spudface' Kartoffel by accident while he was trying to find a cure for elbows. Early uses for the potato include: a lightweight throwing weapon, a cushion for dogs, a cheap alternative to stone, earmuffs for the elderly and most famously as a dangerously unreliable parachute.

In 1954, Harry Mash was the first person to attempt to consume the potato. He died in a horrendous choking accident. Several years later his brother Ron, having picked up his brother's notes, also attempted to eat a potato. He too died, but because of an unrelated steam roller incident. This incident, was how 'mashed potato' was named.

The potato became the vegetable of choice in the 1960's and to be seen without one was the height of 'squareness'. The first human-potato hybrid was born in the mid-seventies and still performs in his local freak show to this day. In the nineties the chipped potato was born. Society has never looked back and now, by law, chips must be served with every meal.

Yes it is all true. I wonder if there was such a thing as a British Potato Council tee shirt (or other British Potato Council goodies) that you happened to have lying around your office. If so, I'd love to own one!

Well done on the potato,

James Spence

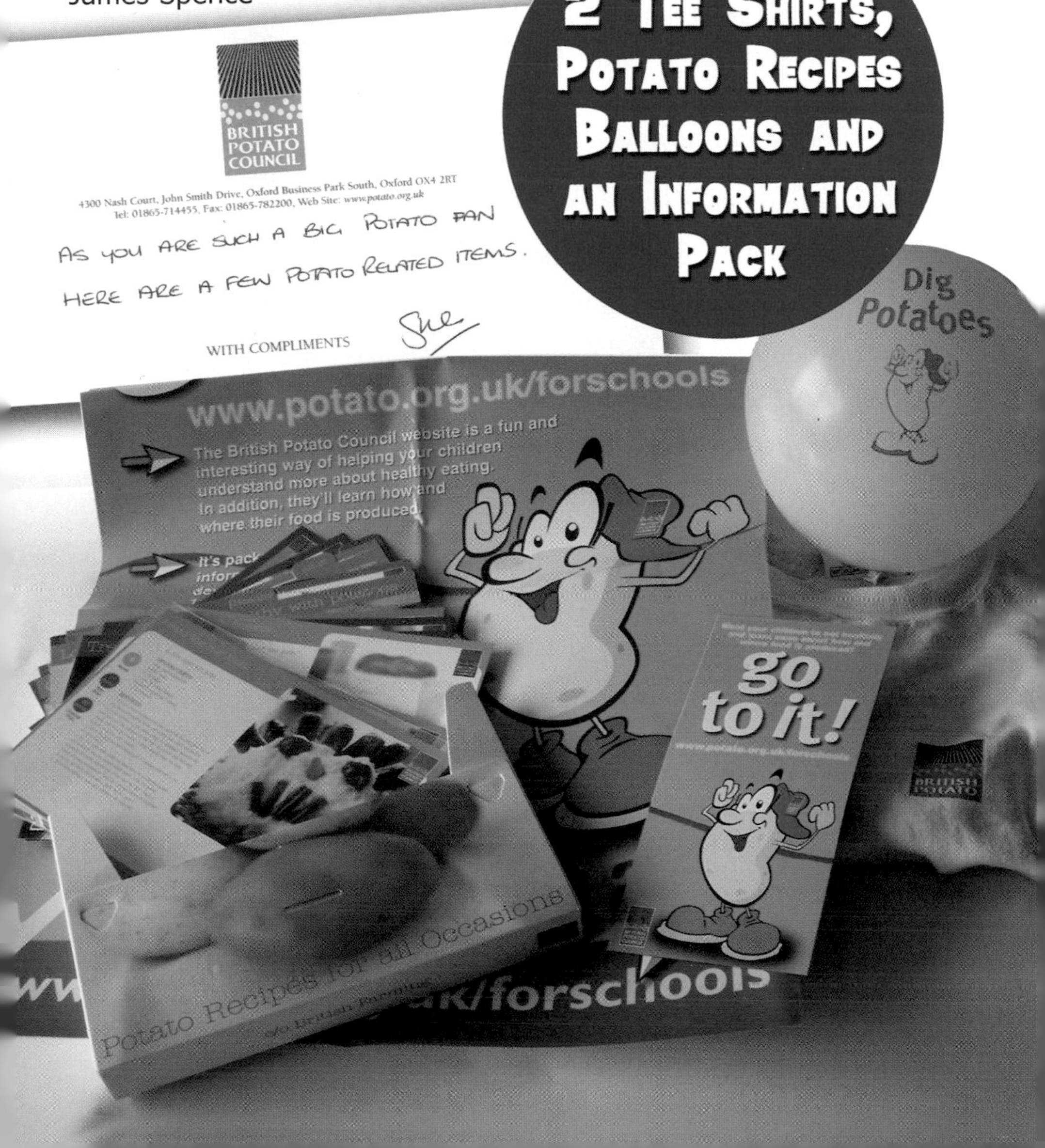
2 Tee Shirts, Potato Recipes Balloons and an Information Pack
BRITISH POTATO COUNCIL
4300 Nash Court, John Smith Drive, Oxford Business Park South, Oxford OX4 2RT
Tel: 01865-714455, Fax: 01865-782200, Web Site: www.potato.org.uk
AS YOU ARE SUCH A BIG POTATO FAN
HERE ARE A FEW POTATO RELATED ITEMS.
Sue
WITH COMPLIMENTS
www.potato.org.uk/forschools
The British Potato Council website is a fun and interesting way of helping your children understand more about healthy eating. In addition, they'll learn how and where their food is produced.
Dig Potatoes
go to it!
Potato Recipes for all Occasions
BRITISH POTATO

To: Adobe
From: James Spence
Subject: What's in a Name?

Hi there,

I've used Adobe products for a long time and find them to be of great quality. Well done on the whole PDF thing. It's marvellous. Light yourselves up a cigar! (or if you don't smoke, take some snuff).

I had a question, however, and it's one that has troubled me for some time. How do you pronounce 'Adobe'. Here are the various options in my eyes:

- A dough bee (as in a bee made from dough)
- A dobby (to rhyme with a jobby)
- A doab (like 'abode' but in tongetwister form)
- Dob (with a silent a and e)
- Jeremy (because I like the name)

If you answer my question I will be satisfied. However, if in addition to providing this answer you send me an Adobe tee shirt, I will be delighted and may well perform a victory dance down my street.

Have a special one,

James Spence

Adobe Systems Europe Limited

Riverside House
502 Gorgie Road
Edinburgh
EH11 3AF
United Kingdom
Phone (44) 131 443 2890
Fax (44) 131 443 2894

Adobe Systems Europe
Customer Services
10/11/04

Dear Mr Spence

Thankyou for your email, it was great to hear your feedback on our products. To answer your question about the company name –
(I knew it had to be from someone resident in Scotland when I read the word jobby!! – our office is in Edinburgh)

If you have access to internet please look at the following site as it gives an audio version of the word Adobe. Your description A dough bee (as in a bee made from dough) was the correct pronunciation.

http://www.m-w.com/cgi-bin/dictionary?book=Dictionary&va=adobe&x=16&y=18

The actual word means –
Function: *noun*
Etymology: Spanish, from Arabic *at-tub* the brick, from Coptic *tObe* brick
1 : a brick or building material of sun-dried earth and straw
2 : a structure made of adobe bricks
3 : a heavy clay used in making adobe bricks; *broadly* **:** alluvial or playa clay in desert or arid regions

I hope you continue to enjoy our products!

Kind regards

AN
ADOBE
PEN

@adobe.com

Customer

dobe.com

Adobe Systems Europe Limited
Riverside House,
502 Gorgie Road, Edinburgh

phone: +44 (131) 443 2890

ps (sorry I don't have any Tshirts at the moment!)

To: McVitie's (Penguin Biscuits)
From: James Spence
Subject: The Way the Cookie Crumbles

Hi there,

Is there anyone out there who doesn't like McVitie's?!! You guys make the best darned biscuits this young man has ever had the pleasure of sampling. You make many varieties of wonderful biscuits and I would love to discuss them all with you, but as a busy man with very little time on my hands, I have elected to discuss with you just one of those biscuit types (details to follow). Word.

You see, crumb assemblers, I have a slightly bizarre tale for you concerning my last visit to the supermarket. Don't stop reading now! I had perused the isles looking for cat biscuits for my little feline friend (Angel). There were a few different cat biscuits to choose from and I picked up one at random (I think it must have been mouse flavoured). As I walked out of the pet food isle, I glanced to the west and saw that there were also dog biscuits available (probably tasted of bone and/or cats). I didn't think much of this, as dog owners are people too, and may wish to reward their dog with a biscuit (perhaps when the dog has learned to body-pop?)

What shocked me to my very soul, however was when I got to the biscuit isle. Yes, I think you know where this is going. On the shelf, right in the middle of the isle, were...

...Penguin biscuits.

Now I don't know much about animal cruelty, but I'd say that people keeping penguins as pets is just plain wrong! And to reward the penguins with a tasty biscuit angers me. What surprised me more was that these biscuits were on the shelf right next to biscuits for human consumption. I assume these Penguin biscuits taste of fish, and I would hate for their fishy aroma to spread onto a nice rich tea or digestive.

This shocking product explains why my local supermarket is constantly over-run with penguins! And why my favourite tee shirt (it had a picture of a halibut on it) was pecked to pieces by the little black and white 'rodents of the north'!

Phew! Take a deep breath, Jamesyboy, and move on...

Anyway, I just wanted to write (a) to alert you to my concerns over your Penguin snacks, (b) because all your other biscuits are fantastic and make break time worth having and (c) to request a (large) McVitie's tee shirt to replace the one those South Pole pests got their peckers on.

Keep up the excellent work, and no more fish-flavoured biscuits please!

James Spence

Mr James Spence

Our Ref : E028681RVG

31st August 2004

Dear Mr Spence

Thank you for contacting us and the complimentary remarks you made concerning our products.

We are always interested to hear our customers' comments and appreciate you taking the time and trouble to contact us, with a truly remarkable tale. You have certainly brightened our day in this office!!!!

Please find enclosed a small token of our appreciation and we hope you enjoy your next purchase of delicious McVitie's biscuits.

Yours sincerely

Mrs Rhonda Gittins
Consumer Services Co-Ordinator

Enc. Voucher £2.00

VOUCHERS TO THE VALUE OF £3.00

PENGUIN goahead! Jaffa Cakes

McVitie's Consumer Services Department, PO Box 7249,
Ashby-de-la-Zouch, Leicestershire LE65 2ZH
T UK 0500 011710 T EIRE 1800 409317 F 01530 411888
E mcvities.consumerservices@unitedbiscuits.com

McVitie's is part of
United Biscuits (UK) Limited.
Registered in England No. 2506007.
Registered Office: Hayes Park,
Hayes End Road, Hayes,
Middlesex, UB4 8EE.

To: Sky TV
From: James Spence
Subject: The Tube

Hi there Broadcasters,

I'm a subscriber to your wonderful satellite organisation: Sky TV. I really enjoy chilling out with a glass of cold lard to watch a bit of telly in the evening. Your excellent service allows me to cram in a good eight hours every night. I also eat.

However, I got to thinking the other day that there are loads of times, such as when I'm asleep, at work or out using my jet pack, when I don't watch any Sky television at all. I'm sure you good people monitor the volume of television that I watch, and would be able to quantify more accurately the amount I've used. As I pay a monthly fee, that means a whole bunch of my Sky is going unwatched. It's almost as if it's being broadcast straight into my dustbin, in a funny kind of way. My favourite food is bacon.

At four o'clock in the morning I woke up in a sweat, my moist face trembling in dusky night. An idea had struck. An amazing idea that would benefit all of mankind. What if the Sky that I didn't use could be shipped out to the poor people of the third world who don't have Sky at all. Not even that rubbish channel with the home decorating on it! It'd be a shame for my unwatched hours to be wasted. I'd even be prepared to deliver the sky overseas myself utilising my mighty jet pack, Trevor. I tend to cut off the fat, so the rest of the bacon is 'pure'.

If this ingenious plan isn't possible, I'd like to switch to plan B, which is thus: Could I get a (large) Sky tee shirt to wear whilst out on one of my jet pack missions. That would be choice. My last tee shirt got covered in bacon fat.

Anyway, keep up the good work compadres.

Come fly with me,

James Spence

To: Budweiser
From: James Spence
Subject: Wassup!

Hey Dudes,

I totally love bud. It's the best drink ever. I drink bud every Friday and Saturday (and sometimes even more frequently than that!) It's a most refreshing beer. I must have spent thousands of pounds on Bud over the years.

Here's a poem I wrote in tribute to your fab beer:

Bud is the greatest. It's the best I've ever had.
I drink it with my friends. I drink it with my Dad.
I drink it in the garden, surrounded by the ants.
I drink it in the evening. I drink it in my pants.
I wish that I had loads of it - enough to cause a flood.
There's nothing better than a glass of cool refreshing bud.

Any chance of a tee shirt for a loyal customer and fan?

Thanks for making Bud,

James Spence

Anheuser-Busch Europe Ltd

Our Ref: 0019859A

September 15, 2004

Mr James Spence

Dear Mr Spence,

Thanks for contacting Anheuser-Busch. We're always delighted to hear from loyal customers. In fact, enthusiastic comments such as yours provide us with the type of feedback necessary to maintain our leadership position in the industry and affirm that we're meeting our customers' needs.

Nothing is more important to us than making a great product for your enjoyment. For more than a century, our story has centred on quality and innovation. Everywhere around the world, Anheuser-Busch brings people together to help them celebrate the good things in life. Your input helps us to enhance our quality assurance efforts and keeps us on track with exceeding customer expectations.

Please accept the enclosed complimentary Anheuser-Busch merchandise as a token of our gratitude for being such a loyal customer. Should you have any additional comments or questions, please don't hesitate to contact us at 0208 332 2302, at the address below or by visiting our website anytime at www.budweiser.co.uk

Again, thank you for your custom and we hope that you will continue to enjoy our products.

Yours sincerely

A Cross.

Annemarie Cross
Consumer Services Manager

Visit us at Budweiser.co.uk / Fresh Beer Tastes Be

To:	Hushpuppies
From:	James Spence
Subject:	Something's Afoot

Hi there,

I had to write to tell you of a problem that I had with a pair of your (usually wonderful) Hush Puppies shoes.

Whilst wearing a pair of your shoes in bed last night, a gentle breeze blew in through the window, lowering the temperature of the room and making me (your customer) feel a little cold. With my free hand, I reached over and grabbed my "sleepy shirt" (a tee shirt that I sleep in when I'm a little cold - it has a snugly bear on the front).

As it was cold I made a (in retrospect rather silly) decision to put my shirt on feet first, i.e. lowering my body through the 'neck' of the tee.

Well, the problem my friends is that the neck wasn't actually as stretchy as I had anticipated, and (you've guessed it, smart reader) the shirt ripped as I put my Hush Puppies shoes through it.

I realise that it wasn't your fault. The shoes were merely the media of my poor shirt's demise, and I, your loyal customer, was responsible for the woeful act. However, I can't help but wonder if it had been a rival firm's shoes, would the outcome have been the same? Would I, in fact, still have the snugly bear's sleepy shirt?

Then it hit me! Hush Puppies must have loads of free promotional tee shirts knocking about! They're one of the best companies in the world after all! So I wondered if we could rebuild the bridge that fell last night? Could you send me a (large) Hush Puppies tee shirt to replace snugly bear? I don't mind if it does not feature a bear.

Here's hoping,

James Spence

Hush Puppies®

Bedtime attire!!

Regards

Julie Bradley
UK MKT. Manager

With Compliments

Hush Puppies (UK) Ltd, 3 The Osiers Office Park, Braunstone, Leicester LE19 1DY.
T: (0116) 281 4300 F: (0116) 281 4360. www.hushpuppies.co.uk
Registered Office: 24 Britton Street, London, EC1M 5UA. Registered in England No

To: eBay
From: James Spence
Subject: I Bid You "Good Day"

Hi eBay,

eBay is the greatest invention since the hat! I love going on to check for Doctor Who bargains, and oh boy have I ever found some! I especially like looking for incorrectly spelt items. That way you have very little competition when bidding for that must-have 8 foot scarf or replica sonic screwdriver!

I have a few suggestions for improving eBay:

- The eBay 'mole': a device that allows users to check out how many other people are watching an item
- The eBay 'coming up page' which lists items that sellers will list up to a year in the future
- 'Honest Harry': A man or program that could 'hold the money' and the item, then once he has BOTH, could issue them out, thereby making fraudulent transactions a thing of the past.
- eBay 'biscuits' - For every thousand transactions, sellers and buyers are rewarded with an eBay biscuit through the post. It's a thought!

Anyway, I also write to congratulate you on being fab, and have composed a brief (but heartfelt) poem:

I love to look on eBay for bargains and for kicks,

I can get rare Doctor Who with only several clicks!

I never need to leave the house. I never need to dress!

I get those timelord goodies with very little stress.

I like to look on eBay while I drink a little juice,

Thanks a million eBay! Though now I'm a recluse!

I would LOVE a large eBay t-shirt. Do you have any for a loyal fan and customer.

Thanks,

James Spence

To: Golden Wonder
From: James Spence
Subject: Wotsit All About?

Hi there Golden Wonder Dudes,

Yesterday there was 'a bit of a situation' involving a packet of your fine crisps. My friend Sebastian and I were playing a game of "Wotsits Shirt Rips", which is a game we invented. The nature of the game is to see who can cram the most Wotsits into their mouth. The winner gets to rip the loser's shirt.

Anyway, Sebastian's score was pitifully small and I took my turn. After an exceptionally brief period of time, I had surpassed his record and I proceeded to rip his shirt, as per the law.

The problem was, however, that HE got mad and to cut a long story short, MY shirt got ripped too!! This is not part of the rules of Wotsits Shirt Rips.

I know that technically none of this is your fault, but at the end of the day, the game is Wotsits Shirt Rips and not some other product. So, I was wondering if you had any Wotsits or Golden Wonder tee shirts that you could send me (and possibly Sebastian)?

Thanks,

James Spence

To:	James Spence
From:	Golden Wonder
Subject:	Re: Wotsit All About?

James,

We do not have any 'specific' Golden Wonder T-Shirts, however I will arrange for a couple of Wheat Crunchies t-shirts to be sent out to you.

Regards,

Zoe

To: Kodak
From: James Spence
Subject: Snap Happy

I wrote a poem in tribute to your wonderful film:

I like to have a giggle. I like to have a laugh.
I like to document it in a lovely photograph.
I love to see my picture in a pretty frame,
And sit back and enjoy, a trip down memory lane.

Do you have a (large) Kodak T-shirt for a loyal fan?
Keep up the good work,

James Spence

To: James Spence
From: Kodak
Subject: Re: Snap Happy

Many thanks for your poem about photography, I must say it went down very well in the office, and I have taken the liberty of passing it onto the Managing Director who always likes to see this kind of thing.

I have put in the post today, a Kodak T-Shirt for your trouble.

Many thanks once again.

Kind regards,

Gill Swift

PR Specialist

To: Disney
From: James Spence
Subject: New Movies

Dear Disney Friends,

I grew up with Disney. The Jungle Book, The Lion King, Mary Poppins, The Black Cauldron and a whole bunch of others (you know your own films for crikey's sake!) For me, Christmas wasn't Christmas unless Uncle Roger was passed out in front of a Disney film, snoring away, his strange mixture of smells (body odour, booze and turnips) filling the room and provoking the rest of the family into furious arguments. Despite it all, the films were a magical escape.

I came up with a few ideas for future Disney films:

- The Last Panda - The story of how the panda became extinct
- Waterface - A story about a boy, his love of swimming and his watery face
- The Lion King 2 - A sequel to the Lion King
- Animated Star Wars - An animated version of the Star Wars films. It could be voiced by the original cast!
- I watched a show about Penguins recently. You could put them in a film.
- The Boy Who Went Off With A Stranger - How about some educational films?
- My cat once got locked in a neighbour's car - That'd be an awesome film. I rescued her.
- Something with a bunch of cute bunnies and bears, etc

Anyway, get back to work, my friends. You've plenty to do with that little list awaiting production. Let me know once they're made and I'll pop along to the cinema to watch them. I heard that some movies make hundreds, even thousands of pounds.

Well, I don't want money for the above ideas. All I want, as a huge fan of your work, is a (large) tee shirt. Do you have such a thing for a loyal fan and film watcher?

Keep up the brilliant work my Disney friends,

James Spence

To: MFI
From: James Spence
Subject: Curl Up and DIY

Hi there Dudes,

What could be finer than a day of sunshine and a browse around MFI? Nothing! That's what!! MFI is a great place to spend time, enjoying the bargains, meeting the friendly staff, taking a 'mock bath' in the store. There's fun to be had in every corner.

I recall on one visit, my wife (Tiffany) and I had a whale of a time playing a fantastic game of hide and seek. I spent about half an hour hiding from my wife in one of your spacious cupboards. In the end, it turned out she'd gone home, but that's not the point. The point is, we had fun. On another occasion we had a great time hiding under the beds and making 'ghost' noises. On a different occasion, we smuggled in a snowman. Not easy in July!

The other day, I was browsing your web site, and when I saw how low the prices were, I dropped the can of sardines I was eating onto myself, ruining my favourite tee shirt (it had a picture of the cast of Knots Landing on it). Now that's low prices!!

Ever thought of extending your range of products to include: Basketball boots? onions? clothes? Just a thought.

Do you have a tee shirt for a loyal fan and customer (I have a gap in my wardrobe following a certain 'low price incident'!)

Thanks a bunch MFI!

James Spence

To: James Spence
From: MFI
Subject: Re: Curl Up and DIY

Good afternoon

Thank you so much for your email. I have forwarded this onto the store, so that they can advise the staff, they haven't got ghosts.

However, we are all intrigued as to where you got the snowman from.

Once again, thank you for taking the time and trouble to pass on your experience.

Kind regards

Maria

E-mail Liaison Team

www.mfi.co.uk

To: Amazon
From: James Spence
Subject: Amazonian Questions

Hi there,

I'm a long-term customer, and a huge fan of Amazon. I've bought loads of stuff from you for many years, even in those early days.

I write with a few ideas to help your business continue to expand:

- Cake vouchers: For every order, a slice of cake. My wife makes lovely cake, and she'd be willing to share recipes
- A cheaper service (but how? I hear you scream) You could have a much more 'risky' service without all this secure server nonsense and where the postage is cheaper because you just attach a stamp and address sticker directly onto the merchandise itself saving perhaps hundreds on postage materials
- Recommendations not based on previous transactions, but based on whether stuff is good or not
- A helpful icon, like that friendly 'paperclip' everyone loves
- Perhaps a catchy tune playing in the background while you surf. If the Cheeky Girls were serenading me as I surfed, you can bet I'd stick around
- If you got your products supplied cheaper, you could pass that cheapness on to the consumer - Solution: smuggling?
- A graduate discount to motivate students not to drop out
- A free tee shirt to anyone who sends in suggestions

I think you can see where this is going now: I would LOVE an Amazon tee shirt. If there was any way this could be arranged I'd be extremely grateful.

Thanks for all you brilliant work. I love shopping at Amazon.

Looking forward to many future purchases,

James Spence

To:	Bernard Matthews
From:	Angel the Cat
Subject:	Gobble It Up

Dear Bernard Matthews

There are several things in life that make me happy. These include being served delicious food, relaxing in the sun, playing in the garden, having my belly rubbed and sitting on James. It is this last one that brings me the most joy! James is very kind and strokes me while I sit on him.

I have noticed a trend. If James is happy, then he is more likely to let me sit on him. It's true! So, I try to do what I can to make James happy. This includes rubbing myself against his legs, bringing him dead animals, looking cute and keeping myself clean.

However, the thing that makes James happiest of all is snacking on some delicious turkey. So I wanted to write to you to say how much I appreciate your fruit, as James's happiness is very important to me. If you have any Bernard Matthews tee shirts or other cool promotional stuff, I know James would be delighted and would let me sit on him all night long!

Thanks very much. Purr...

Angel the Cat

1st March 2007

Angel Spence

VOUCHERS TO THE VALUE OF £2.00

Dear Angel

Thank you for your recent email.

We were delighted to learn how much James enjoys our Turkey, and how this in turn makes you happy.

It is always good to learn that people (and cats) are getting pleasure from our products.

Unfortunately we do not have any T-shirts or promotional 'stuff' available at this time to send to James.

However we are enclosing some complimentary vouchers for £2.00 to enable James to purchase one of our products, which will hopefully make him happy, and in doing so he will allow you to sit on his lap and rub your belly (the thing which brings you the most joy).

We really were impressed that you were able to send email, and we would like to thank you for taking the time to contact us.

Yours Sincerely
For **BERNARD MATTHEWS FOODS LTD**

p.p.

KAREN ANTHONY
CONSUMER RELATIONS MANAGER

telephone: +44(0)1603 872611 head office fax: +44(0)1603 871118 factory/sales fax: +44(0)1603 872421
Bernard Matthews Foods Ltd., Great Witchingham Hall, Norwich, Norfolk NR9 5QD, United Kingdom Registered No. 1831006

To: Cadbury
From: James Spence
Subject: Chocolate Poetry

Hi there,

I just wanted to write and say how much I enjoy your chocolate. I must have spent thousands of pounds on Cadbury's products over the years and every penny is well spent. I really enjoy your chocolate bars, especially Dairy Milk, Fudge and Caramel bars.

I wrote a poem in tribute to your tasty snacks:

Let's hear it for Dairy Milk, the greatest ever snack.
I wish I had hundreds (enough to fill a sack),
Every bite I take is better than the last,
Until the bar is finished, then I wish I was in the past!

Do you have a (large) Cadbury's T-shirt for a loyal fan?

Cheers,

James Spence

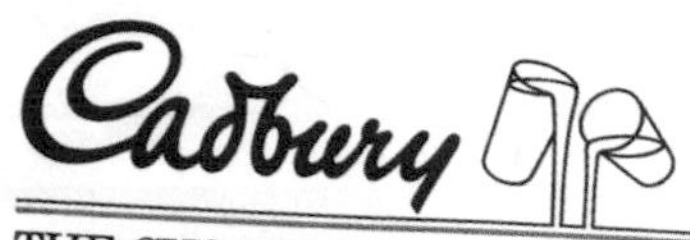

THE CHOCOLATE. THE TASTE.

CADBURY LTD.

PO BOX 12
BOURNVILLE
BIRMINGHAM B30 2LU
CONSUMER DIRECT LINE 0121-451 4444
SWITCHBOARD TELEPHONE 0121-458 2000
FAX No. 0121-451 4297
http://www.cadbury.co.uk

30 July 2004

Mr James Spence

BASEBALL CAP AND KEYRING

Our Ref:- 1086830A

Dear Mr Spence,

Thank you for your recent E mail.

I enjoyed reading you poem, unfortunately, we do not have any t shirts at present that I could send to you. However I hope you will accept the enclosed gift with our best wishes.

Thank you again for contacting us.

Yours sincerely

Helen Franklin
Consumer Relations Department

Registered in England. Company No. 155256 ... 30 2LU

To: Vileda
From: James Spence
Subject: Absorbing Message

Greetings to you Good Citizens,

I am James Spence, mild mannered email writer and doer of good deeds. Recently I was bitten by a radioactive sponge, transforming me from a normal everyday member of the public into The Mighty Spongemaster (TM), righter of wrongs and custodian of virtue!

As The Mighty Spongemaster, I look just like an ordinary member of the public, except my entire torso is made out of Sponge! I'm no biologist and don't know how I have survived, but rest assured I have, and I'm fighting on the side of the good guys!

With my remarkable Sponge powers I am capable of performing the following amazing deeds:

- Soaking up liquids
- Standing on the spot for lengthy periods of time (ideal for surveillance)
- Assimilating information quickly (a sponge for knowledge)
- Becoming a comfortable cushion for haemorrhoid sufferers
- Absorbing bullets, yes bullets
- Wearing spandex underpants and a wig
- Fighting such villains as: Hoodwink, The Spill Hound and Fizzo the Clown.

But, good people, you are probably wondering why I am jeopardising my greatest secret (Who I am). It is for one simple reason, my friends. Read on...

I require a superhero outfit. Yes, in order to protect my identity and save the world, I require only one thing... a tee shirt, and what better way to show the likes of Hoodwink and his Henchmen that I'm full of energy, than a Vileda tee shirt?

Can you send a (large) Vileda tee shirt? In return, I will protect the world from the likes of the nefarious Spill Hound.

Reach for the skies,

James 'Mighty Spongemaster' Spence

To: James Spence
From: Vileda
Subject: Re: Absorbing Message

Further to your recent mail below, unfortunately, we do not have any Vileda T-shirts, will a pen do??!!!

Linda

To: Vileda
From: James Spence
Subject: Re: Absorbing Message

Hi Linda,

A pen would be fantastic!! Thanks very much. Keep up the good work,

James

To: James Spence
From: Vileda
Subject: Re: Absorbing Message

On its way - just keep Fizzo the Clown out of my way...

PEN AND "BOP WHILE YOU MOP" TAPE

To: Lucozade
From: James Spence
Subject: Energy Drinks

Greetings to you Good Citizens,

I am James Spence, mild mannered email writer and doer of good deeds. Recently I was bitten by a radioactive herring, transforming me from a normal everyday member of the public into Herring-Chap(TM), righter of wrongs!

With my remarkable Herring powers I am capable of performing the following amazing deeds:

- Jumping quite high, I'd say about two feet
- Running really fast
- Stopping to gather breath following the above events
- Pointing at nice looking flowers
- Deliberately spelling words rong
- Foaming at the mouth when bitten by rabid monkeys
- Wearing spandex underpants and a wig
- Fighting such villains as: Hoodwink, The Snowclone and Fizzo the Clown

But, good people, you are probably wondering why I am jeopardising my secret identity. It is for one simple reason my friends. I have no superhero outfit. I require a tee shirt in order to protect my alter-ego.

Please can you send me a (large) Lucozade tee shirt, and I will protect the world from the likes of the nefarious Hoodwink.

Reach for the skies,

James 'Herring-Chap' Spence

NO REPLY

To:	British Board of Film Classification
From:	James Spence
Subject:	Rate It

Dear British Board of Film Classification,

THIS EMAIL IS RATED U: SUITABLE FOR ALL

I've been watching films ever since I got my sight back (long story, in which the moral is 'don't throw a dart directly upwards and watch to see where it lands'). Your excellent classification system has certainly informed my decision making process about what sort of films I like to watch (I'm strictly a '12A' man).

Excuse my slightly jokey writing style. I suffer from a condition called 'Shinkler's Arm'.

Anybum, the real reason I write is because although I appreciate the current system detailing if a film is suitable for a specific age-group, I wondered if you planned to expand your criteria, i.e. will there ever be a film classification to identify if a film is a load of old unwatchable guff? Why not call this category 'Titanic'? Let me know what you think.

I also write because I was curious about how you rate an 18 film? Do you show it to a 17 year-old then sit back and wait to see if he becomes traumatised?

Finally I write because as a huge movie merchandise collector, I wondered if you happened to have a British Board of Film Classification tee shirt (ideally large) that you could send me to start off my new collection, or failing that, any other cool British Board of Film Classification stuff (such as a pen?). It would take pride of place in my collection.

Many thanks for your attention,

James Spence

Suitable for all
May be unsuitable for children under 8
12A may be unsuitable for children under 12 Children under 12 must be accompanied by an adult
Suitable only for 15 years and over
Suitable only for adults
Pens, Pencils, Mousemats Posters, Postcards and The Annual Report
New film classification symbols
bbfc
British Board of Film Classification
annua
www.bbfc.co.uk

To: British Dental Association
From: James Spence
Subject: All Smiles

Dear Dentists,

I don't understand all the fuss people make about healthy teeth. I have for a long time suspected that dentistry is a scam, and wanted to email you to share my opinion and invite you to address my concerns. That is, if you can. The following arguments contain some pretty damning evidence, so you might not want the world at large to see them.

First off, everyone's teeth fall out by the time they reach thirty. Fact. So what's the point of going to a dentist?!! You're just putting off the inevitable. I am only 28, so I still have 2 teeth. One for biting and one for chewing. In 2 years time I'll be shot of them for good. Good riddance to bad rubbish I say. They're only holding me back.

As a man of the cloth (I'm a window cleaner), I can appreciate the value of keeping valuable stuff clean, like windows, but teeth?! They come free with your body. No cost means no value.

In the event that your teeth fall out (or as mine did, go 'bendy') you can get an even better set made for you. Rich people can even have gold dentures made. Unfortunately this has the down side of making their faces heavy and hard to lift.

In the future, they'll make technologically advanced dentures with enhanced features that normal teeth don't have, such as an AM/FM radio, compass or egg whisk. Once these puppies hit the shops normal teeth will be a thing of the past.

Dentists take your money but never do any research with it. I mean, why not invest some of your cash inventing a cream for your teeth that you could apply every night to keep them healthy. If such a thing existed, I know I'd use it.

If you have an information pack, or any thoughts on 'dental cream', I would love you to send them to me. Better yet, if you had a free British Dental Association tee shirt, my mind would be completely turned around on the subject.

Keep smiling,

James Spence

To: Google
From: James Spence
Subject: Search Me

Hi there,

Google is the engine that helps me every day,
When searching on the web, I always find my way.
Google lets me do my favourite things in my life.
I download lots of music. It's how I met my wife.
Tiff and I've been married for very near a year,
If it weren't for Google, I would not know my dear.
Our 1st anniversary's in August and I have a small request
You can mull it over and do what you think best,
I'd like a Google t-shirt. I'll give it to the missus,
That's a guaranteed way to ensure more of her kisses!
I'm grateful for all you do. You are the greatest engine,
Thanks to you and all you do (and thanks for your attention)

Thanks Google. If you did happen to have a (large) tee shirt, I'd be thrilled (and so would Tiffany)

Thanks,

James Spence

2 Tee Shirts Plus This Poem was Published in a Book about Google

To: Sunday Mail
From: James Spence
Subject: Hero's Tale

Greetings Good Citizens,

It is I, the Mighty SpongeMaster, doer of good deeds, righter of wrongs, custodian of virtue, browser of newspapers and saviour or the world via the medium of sponge.

As a superhero, I don't get much time off, but when I do have a little time, I like to hang up my cape and poncho and settle down in front of your marvellous newspaper and have a read! Using my Sponge-powers I can absorb a lot of information in very little time. It is such a good read, I wanted to write an email to say how excellent the Sunday Mail is. I absorb every word!

However, disaster struck the other week. Read on, my friends, read on.

I was reading the Sunday Mail after an arduous battle saving society! Thankfully I prevailed and Hoodwink and his Henchmen were locked out of harm's way for good. I had changed into my civilian clothes (jeans, my favourite tee shirt, thick black glasses to conceal my identity etc). However, after all my efforts I was exhausted, and unusually for me, fell asleep whilst reading the paper.

When I awoke, I discovered that my favourite tee shirt (it had a picture of a polar bear in the snow on it) was covered in newspaper ink. The previously near-white shirt was ruined. Even after numerous washes, it was seriously discoloured. I guess there's always a price to pay when saving humanity. "Hoodwink! Will your tyranny ever end?!!"

Suddenly a thought struck! My good friends at the Sunday Mail may have a (large) tee shirt for a loyal reader to replace the one I lost saving the world from Hoodwink. What say you, chums?

Thanks for a great read every day,

The Mighty SpongeMaster

To: Fisherman's Friend
From: James Spence
Subject: Good Eatin'

Hi there Befrienders of the Humble Fishfinder,

I am a chap who loves Fisherman's Friend. Fisherman's Friends are perhaps the greatest fisherman-related product the world has ever seen. Better than beards. And massive wellies? Don't make me laugh!! I've never met a Fisherman in the wild, but I dare say if I did, I'd like to shake him by the hand (paw?)

I digress.

This email has been sent to you because I needed to get something off my chest. Yes, I am a Fisherman's Friend fan, but I'm afraid I have a tragic 'Fisherman's Friend' story to tell...

Let me set the scene: I live with my friend Sebastian (a doctor), normally a pretty decent sort. At the time of this fine story, He and I were watching a particularly good episode of Doctor Who (it was an Ice Warrior story) when suddenly hunger struck. I asked Sebastian if he was hungry but he didn't answer, so engrossed was he in the episode - he's a Who nut!

I got up and headed for the fridge to see what I could get to quash those hunger pains. The fridge was largely empty: a few cans of lager, some eggs, prunes, chilli sauce and punnet of lard. However, right at the back, under my journals, was a pack of Fisherman's Friend that I had not even realised I owned (I like my Trouthunter's Buddies cold)!

Thinking my luck was in, I promptly poured the Fisherman's Friends down my gullet with a grin. I then returned to Sebastian and our Doctor Who marathon, telling him that I'd killed my hunger via the medium of the Friend of the Fisherman. This is where the story goes downhill...

Sebastian didn't so much as speak to me upon my return. It transpired that the Fisherman's Friends I had enjoyed so vivaciously, were his and it was not my place to devour it so greedily.

The fight that ensued was not one that I will discuss in detail but, needless to say, it was pretty wild and my favourite tee shirt (it had a picture of a potato in underpants on it) was destroyed by fire. The remainder of a tuna sandwich was smeared into our cactus.

Sebastian has not spoken to me since and I still don't know if the Doctor saved the world from the Ice Warriors, as Sebastian has hidden the DVD. Delicious snacks are a good thing, but not worth losing a good friend and tee shirt over.

I realise that there is nothing you can do to restore my friendship with Sebastian, but I wondered if you happened to have a spare Fisherman's Friend tee shirt lying around to replace the shirt I lost in the incident described above.

Thanks so much for the fantastic treats. I even enjoy them on a sandwich!! You guys do a brilliant job.

Well done all of you,

James Spence

To: James Spence
From: Fisherman’s Friend
Subject: Re: Good Eatin’

Dear Mr. Spence,

I am replying to your enquiry sent to the Fisherman's Friend web site as Impex Management Co Ltd are the Sales and Marketing Manager for Lofthouse of Fleetwood Ltd (the manufacturers of Fisherman's Friend products) world-wide. Many thanks for your message sent to the Fisherman's Friend web site.

This is truly an unusual and sad story but I am completely bemused, is the FISHERMAN'S FRIEND you are referring to the alcoholic drink that is manufactured in Denmark, if so Lofthouse of Fleetwood Ltd are not the manufacturers of this product. I ask this question being as it is very unlikely that FISHERMAN'S FRIEND lozenges would be kept in a fridge and you do mention ‘pouring it down your throat’.

If what you are referring to is the alcoholic drink unfortunately, although we are aware of this product, I am not aware who the manufacturers are, so I can’t help you any further.

Regards

Sue Brown

To: Fisherman’s Friend
From: James Spence
Subject: Re: Good Eatin’

Hi Sue,

I was not aware of the drink. I was in fact referring to your very tasty lozenges. They are indeed kept in the fridge because I like them cold. In fact I am surprised that other people don't keep them in the fridge as they are really, really yummy when served chilled. The 'pouring' down my throat was merely a metaphor for the rate at which I consumed those tasty cold treats!

I would absolutely love a Fisherman's Friend tee shirt and if such a thing exists I would be thrilled to own one. It would be the pride of my wardrobe and I'm sure would attract many admiring glances.

Many thanks my friend,

James Spence

To: James Spence
From: Fisherman's Friend
Subject: Re: Good Eatin'

Dear James,

As we have distributors in each country who arrange their own advertising and promotions we do not really have promotional items here, but I will have a furridge and see what I can do but you have to give me a few days, but I assure you I won't forget.

Also if you advise me what flavour lozenges Sebastian prefers I will send you some for him and hopefully this will go some way to restoring you friendship.

Regards

Sue

To:	Pampers
From:	James Spence
Subject:	Snug

Hi there,

I find your easy-up pants most comfortable.

Please can you send me a Pampers tee shirt. or vouchers for more wonderful Pampers products?

Thanks,

James Spence

To: Discovery Foods
From: James Spence
Subject: Spice Up Your Life

I just wanted to write and say how much I enjoy your foods. I must have spent thousands of pounds on Discovery foods over the years and every penny is well spent. I always like a Mexican meal, and must confess I rarely eat much else!

I wrote a poem in tribute to your wonderful food:

Let's make the world a spicy place, it sounds like a great plan.
Let's eat jalapeños and chilli from the pan.
Rejoice in enchiladas, tortillas and refried beans.
I'll eat Discovery foods, until I can't fit in my jeans!

Do you have a (large) Discovery T-shirt for a loyal fan?

Cheers,

James Spence

To: James Spence
From: Discovery Foods
Subject: Re: Spice Up Your Life

James,

Thank you for your email and please accept my sincere apologies for the delay in responding. I enjoyed reading your email, its good to know we have such loyal, poetic and crazy customers out there! Thank you for taking the time to contact us to tell us how much you enjoy our product range.

I am sorry to say that we do not produce any t-shirts but we have Discovery t-towels that we will send you to the address below along with some complimentary BBQ products for you to sample. We have an entire new range of BBQ products out in Sainsburys, Tesco and Waitrose stores so hopefully you will enjoy these just as much as our other products.

I look forward to hearing your feedback. Keep up the excellent poem writing!!

Regards,

Paula

To: Bounty
From: James Spence
Subject: The Greatest Name of All!

Hi there,

I'm a huge fan of Bounty and all your good work. Yours is a wonderful and generous organisation. Well done to all of you. Time for an office Mexican wave, I'd say.

However, I regret I have to write with a small concern. You see, I was having a look through your (fantastic) web site and noticed something that enraged me to my very soul (a little). It caused me to rip off my favourite tee shirt (it had a dancing munchkin on it) in what could only be described as a blind fury. (If you've read what my name is, you've probably already guessed)

That's right.

I clicked into your section called the "Top 100 most popular Baby Names" and noticed that MY name (James) was only Fourth on the list. Fourth?!!! I've never felt so unpopular. Fourth is simply not good enough! And to add insult to injury, James came in after Jack, Joshua (is that even a real name?) and Thomas. Pretty poor, I think you'll agree, James-fans.

As a very competitive man, I need to be the best, to beat the rest and give my life zest - ain't no pest! Therefore I suggest that next to 'James' on your list, you put in a hyperlink to the following statement:

"Greetings soon-to-be-parents. You are currently considering names for your child. By clicking the hyperlink to this message you have indicated that 'James' is a potential candidate for your child, and as such you are a person of good taste, style and sophistication. 'James', a beautiful sounding name, has a number of advantages over other children's names:

- It sounds somehow ...heroic

- It rhymes with 'names' and 'games', meaning your child could be Subject: to a number of poems and limericks
- James is a very calming name. Ahhh.
- With a 'J' in the mix, a high Scrabble score is assured
- There are no swear words that rhyme with James, except possibly "butt-flames"
- By naming your child James, you are giving him options. He could go by any of the following identities: Jim, Jimmy, Jimbo, Jamesy, Jamesycakes, Jim Lad, Jamesorama, Jimbob, The Mighty Spongemaster or Jamie
- James is also a good name for girls
- People called James have the best tee shirts
- If your surname is Bond, your child will be the coolest kid in school
- Every Tom, Dick and Harry is called Jack, Joshua and Thomas
- It is the same first name as Paul McCartney
- I like it

Go on, parent pick 'James' and give your child a fair start in life."

Bounty. I thank you for this opportunity to enhance my name's position in the list.

Can I trouble you for one more thing (in fact the whole point of the email if truth be told). As I ripped my favourite tee shirt upon my discovery that I'm (so far) only fourth on the list, I wondered if you happened to have a (large) Bounty tee shirt you could send a loyal fan?

I love Bounty,

James Spence

To: James Spence
From: Bounty
Subject: Re: The Greatest Name of All!

Dear James

Thank you for your email and your extremely kind comments about Bounty.com.

The Bounty Baby Names Poll is conducted annually. It comprises the names of around 97% of all newborns that year. Our Data Analysis team then run the statistics to produce the poll. In accordance with the Market Research Society best practice guidelines, and to ensure impartiality, Bounty cannot be seen to favour some names above others. Therefore, we cannot implement the hyperlink you suggest.

The choice of names is a personal matter for parents. However, trends do appear from time to time - often as a result of cultural or social exposure of a particular name. The sources of influence are many and varied.

Although it is kind of you to suggest that Bounty.com might be one of them, in truth, if you want to increase the number of other number of other babies called 'James', you should consider focusing your energies and talents on becoming a media celebrity or a sports star. Another method might be to write a best-selling novel, or screen play, and name the dashing hero 'James'. (Ian Fleming enjoyed great success through this route.)

Alternatively you could try and become a King. We wish you the best of luck with your endeavours.

Finally, we are sorry to tell you that there is no such thing as a Bounty t-shirt, so we are unable to send you one. Thank you for taking the time to write to Bounty.

Best wishes

Bounty Customer Services

To: DSL Northwest
From: James Spence
Subject: Greetings From Scotland

Hi there Chaps,

Greetings from Scotland. I am a Scottish Internet user who keeps hearing about DSL Northwest. However, I believe you only operate in the USA. Just my luck to be on the wrong side of the Atlantic! Any plans to open a venture over here? Anyway, it's rhymin' time:

DSL Northwest: What a super bunch,
They're better than a lager! They're better than my lunch!
I wish that I could use them. They sound good enough for me!
But curse my rotten luck, I'm in the wrong country!

I don't suppose you'd send a (large) tee shirt over to the UK for me to wear and promote your services over here in Europe?

All the best,

James Spence

To: Richard and Judy
From: James Spence
Subject: Ideas for Richard's Show

Hi there,

SHOW SUGGESTIONS FOR THE NEW SERIES

Love the show, guys. I wondered if you had a Richard and Judy tee shirt for a devoted viewer? I wouldn't expect one just for free! No sir, I will earn it by suggesting the following items for the show for that happy day when it returns to our screens:

Stunt of the Day: Richard could do a stunt (starting with smaller stunts like abseiling and skiing but working up to lion taming, blindfold motorcycle stunts, etc). It would be very exciting and would be brilliant for end-of-series clip compilations and future reminiscence shows.

Computer Games Review: This is really for the mums rather than the kids. The kids know all about what games they want, but let's face it chumps, the games are not always suitable for the younger consumer. How about Richard plays the games then lets the viewer know whether they're any good or are too violent for our children (or ourselves)? If it's good enough for Richard, it's good enough for this young man.

Bird-watching with Bill Oddie: Richard could go out bird-watching with Bill Oddie (who let's face it should be on television EVERY day). Bill could give information to Richard before these segments get filmed so that they could share bird-chat on an equal footing. Otherwise Bill may come across as a bit of a know-it-all and Richard, just a knuckleheaded follower - whose show is this?!!

Richard's story-time: Richard could read a chapter of a book every day. It would probably be best if he read from the same book each day, and kept the chapters in the same sequence they appear in the book.

Richard's chips guide: Ever noticed how chips are not a constant in this life? Different vendors of the chipped potato put their own slant on them, often with dire consequences. Richard could try out chips in a different restaurant every day, perhaps talking to other customers about their chip experiences. Maybe Bill Oddie could muscle in on this one too?

Advice from experience, not facts: They could listen to what the viewers problems are and instead of some fly-by-night doctor, lawyer or agony aunt offering solutions, how about Richard pops in a few. That's who the show is all about after all.

You guys put on a brilliant show. If you have a Richard and Judy tee shirt, I would wear it every day and would send you a photo of me in it (perhaps Richard might show it on the programme?).

Thanks a million,

James Spence

To: Hewlett Packard
From: James Spence
Subject: Print

Hi there Printer People,

I have been a customer of HP various times. Your printers are always a joy to see.

A thought struck me the other day as I wandered around the grounds of my flat. Wouldn't it be awesome to own a HP tee shirt? I would call it Cuthbert we would have some great times together:

- We'd go to the zoo. Cuthbert loves the tigers.
- Watch Richard and Judy on telly. I like Richard, but Cuthbert prefers Judy.
- Enter the Olympics - Cuthbert would fuel my desire to win
- Destroy evil - We'd be an ace crime fighting team
- Invent a new type of beer glass, four times larger than a normal one (not for use by people with brittle easily snapped necks).

Therefore, for the good of humanity itself, could you send me a (large) Cuthbert. He'd have a lovely home.

Thanks,

James Spence

Hewlett-Packard Limited
Cain Road
Bracknell
Berkshire RG12 1HN
www.hp.com/uk

Cuthbert the HP T-shirt

Dear James

Thank you for contacting HP and your kind words about our printers.

Please find enclosed an HP t-shirt, size large, and a cosy HP ski scarf. The winds off the North Sea can be a bit nippy in the winter time.

May I wish you all many happy hours together.

With kind regards

Katie

Katie Clements

To:	Panasonic
From:	James Spence
Subject:	Jamesonic

Greetings Panasonic People,

As I drive to and from work each day, I like to listen to a jaunty tune. Amongst my favourite artists are the Doors, Led Zeppelin, Bob Marley, Tom Waits, the Who, David Bowie, Lou Reed and Peter Gabriel. As I'm sure you'll agree, artists of this calibre require a pretty decent stereo in order to do justice to these pumpin' beats, and I'm happy to report that my Panasonic does not disappoint.

Just last week, I found myself in a traffic jam en route to the 'meat clinic' with only a collection of thumping tunes to keep me company. Normally a traffic jam results in misery on my part, but on this occasion with Bowie on the stereo, I felt somewhat frivolous and came up with the following ways to avoid the traffic jam blues, only one of which I actually did. See if you can guess which one:

- Amuse the other drivers with an impromptu improvisation of 'Les Mis'
- Arrange the debris that lies around your car into order of colour, creating a spectrum of crap
- Point at the sky, looking worried, and raise your meteor shields
- Find out how caring the other drivers are by faking a heart attack
- Re-enact the Big Bang
- Write 'Anguish' down the side of your car in gravy
- Check your mirror to make sure you are confident of your vampire status

- Put a sign in the window of your car saying 'Mobile Massage Parlour Open For Business'
- Accelerate at full throttle shouting "banzai!"
- Relax and have a beer
- Hide from the other drivers for ten minutes then jump up and shout "Last one in the glove compartment smells of baboon."
- Discover your bovine qualities
- Turn to the dark side (or light side depending what side you were on to begin with)
- Think up clever ways of exacting your ruthless revenge on the evil Bertie Steinbeck
- Shoot out the tyres of the other cars just like in the movies but without the hassle of a car chase
- Just like in the A-Team, convert your car into a war machine
- Finger a bun
- Pretend you are in a broken driving simulator
- Summon up the spirit of Elvis for a gig
- Listen to some fantastic music on the Panasonic radio

I feel that in order to perform the above activities to the best of my abilities I would need an outfit that matches the quality of my stereo and therefore, you wonderful people, I would like to request a (large) Panasonic tee shirt. I would be most grateful and would give it (her?) a good home.

Special handshakes,

James Spence

To: Felix
From: James Spence
Subject: Cat Treats

Greetings Purrrr-veyors of Cat Treats,

Angel the cat (often referred to as 'the Beast' by my wife and I) LOVES your sachets of cat treats. We often find ourselves of an evening attempting to coax her in from outside (we've never let her stay out all night for fear of her getting lost / hungry / lured on to a giant catapult by old man Jenkins, our cat-detesting neighbour, and twanged across the village). Normally the ONLY way the Beast will willingly return inside is by our shaking a tub of Felix cat treats in her general direction. She's a sucker for those cat treats! What's in them? Lager?

It is with Angel's love of Felix cat treats in mind that I write.

I like to watch an episode of 'Doctor Who' in the evening while my wife (Tiffany) writes up her 'fridge journals'. I found myself deeply engrossed in the show (it was the one with the Drashigs) and forgot all about our little Beast. When the episode finished, the Doctor was left in his usual end-of-episode cliff-hanger situation, but what I didn't expect when I looked out the window, was to see Angel the cat in a similar predicament!

The Beast had somehow got locked INSIDE old man Jenkins car!

Now, as it happens Jenkins is not a lover of cats and has been quite vocal about his distaste for our little Angel "If I catch that pest near my garden, I'll pelt it with sprouts," he claimed. Her surprise appearance inside his beloved vintage automobile was therefore not a laughing matter.

I immediately ran outside to let the cat out and discovered that all the doors were locked. Angel had locked herself inside his car!! I found myself wondering 'why would the Beast go anywhere near old man Jenkins car?' Then I noticed on the back seat a tub IDENTICAL to the one we keep Angel's cat treats in.

The mystery was solved but it still left the dilemma of how to get the cat out of a hostile locked sports car.

Old man Jenkins vehicle is a convertible with a soft top, and as luck would have it, there was a small gap in the sunroof, a gap just big enough to lower something into. I climbed onto the roof of the car, took off my tee shirt, lowered it down through the gap and around the door locking mechanism. With a tug (and an unpleasant ripping sound), the door unlocked itself. Needless to say, my favourite tee shirt (it has a picture of an enraged monkey on it) was destroyed.

Before I left Jenkins car, I couldn't resist looking inside that tub which was so similar to our 'Felix cat treats' tub, and do you know what was inside?

...sprouts!

I appreciate that my destroyed tee shirt is nothing to do with Felix. Your fine organisation has been a beacon of joy to the beast from the east. However, I am down one tee shirt. I therefore wondered if you happened to have any Felix tee shirts that I could proudly wear when rescuing the cat from such bizarre situations as detailed above.

Thanks very much, and thanks for making the greatest cat treats. We'd be lost without them!

James Spence

Mr James Spence

13/08/04

Our Reference: 10276849/669906

Dear Mr Spence

Thank you for contacting us with Angel's predicament and for your very kind comments about Felix Rascal's Rewards.

First, may we say how pleased we are to hear that Angel enjoys this brand so much. It has always been our company policy to manufacture products of the highest possible quality and it is therefore gratifying when customers such as yourself tell us of their satisfaction and their pets' enjoyment.

We are pleased to enclose a T-shirt for you and some treats for Angel, a long with some vouchers to go towards some free Felix Rascal's Rewards, which we hope you will accept with our compliments.

We are always glad to receive comments from our customers and may we thank you again for taking the time to contact us. If we can be of further assistance please contact us again on the above telephone number.

Yours sincerely

Lorna

Lorna Lawson
Pet Care Advisor

Purina PetCare Service, P.O. Box 297, New Malden, Surrey KT3 4WL
Tel: (UK) 0871 230 2325 (ROI) 012 477 705 Fax: 0870 2414153

TEE SHIRT
AND
CAT TREATS
TOP CAT
TOP CAT
felix
PURINA
felix
Chicken
flavour
CHEWY TREATS

To: Kwik Bite Sandwich Shop
From: James Spence
Subject: Sandwiches Untombed

Dear Kwik Bite (Dunfermline's Greatest Sandwich Shop),

I have amazing news for you! News which will thrill you to your very pantaloons or further! News which could transform the way in which you market your business!

Sandwich Maker, you may already know my name. Yes, I am THE James Spence, Britain's premier Archaeologist (voted "Best Newcomer" in Dig Magazine's 2002 reader's poll, although this award was later revoked due to certain irregularities concerning vote tampering and voter cloning).

Several months ago, on a dig in Cairo, Egypt, France, I made the discovery of a lifetime! I had, quite by chance, uncovered the tomb of an ancient pharoh known only as Tutenparparp, out in the desert. The tomb was breathtaking and spectacular, and filled with incredible hieroglyphics and treasures beyond imagination. You'd have loved it, Sandwich Builder. It was special.

I spent several hours documenting the contents of the tomb and drawing the strange scribblings on the walls. Some of the more unusual items in the tomb included: a barbeque set, a false nose (glass), a jar of what looked like pickled eggs (but I'm sure must have been something else) and assorted unicorn faces. These amazing items were to completely transform our understanding of ancient Egyptian culture.

Unfortunately, Sandwich Creator, the story does not end well as when I entered the tomb, I hadn't checked to see if anyone had followed me. It was a mistake I will regret for the rest of my days. Unbeknownst to me, I had indeed been followed into the tomb. By a giraffe. And it was hungry.

The giraffe immediately started eating mummies and treasure, and even started licking the priceless hieroglyphics off the wall. Before long, the discovery of the century was entirely devoured.

Even the pyramid outside ended up in its remarkable belly. I was lucky to escape with my life, but not before it had consumed my lucky tee shirt.

Stuffed, the giraffe waddled away, leaving all evidence that the tomb had ever existed destroyed. All that was left were my memories and the drawings and notes I had taken.

Over the next few months I set to work analysing the strange symbols I had copied that fateful day in Egypt, France. This is where the most remarkable part of the story begins. You see, Sandwich Composer, the symbols turned out to be co-ordinates. Specifically, they were the co-ordinates of your Sandwich Shop: Kwik Bite in Dunfermline, Scotland, France.

No wonder your sandwiches are so tasty! They've been blessed by Egyptian Pharohs! Yowzah!

Of course, upon making this amazing discovery, I simply had to share it with you, my pharoh-friendly Sandwich Constructor.

The sad part of the story, of course, is that as a result of my dig, I lost my favourite tee shirt (it said "Archaeologists Dig It Slowly" on the back). What a tragedy! But this is where you could help, Sandwich Legend. Perhaps you have a Kwik Bite tee shirt you could send to me? I promise to keep it out of reach of hungry giraffes.

I look forward to your reply,

James Spence

To: James Spence
From: Kwik Bite
Subject: Re: Sandwiches Untombed

Dear James,

Sorry to hear that you're in a jam over the loss of your tee-shirt. The giraffe experience must have been terrifying.

Had the letter come from someone without your exemplary credentials we might have put the giraffe story down to being a tall tale – sorry, should that have been tail?

Here at Kwik Bite we are preoccupied with food. We aren't Dunfermline's Tastiest Takeaway for nothing, but tee-shirts we don't have. We have tea, but the closest it comes to a shirt is when someone spills it over theirs.

We aren't too surprised that you found an Egyptian hieroglyphic reference to us as we make delicious sand-wiches (get it?) and the Pharoahs must have got the word.

It may go some way to lifting your spirits to know that the next time you visit our humble premises, a free cup of tea, freshly made, like all our tasty products, will be available just for you. In fact, we'll also give you one of our delicious breakfast boxes to set you up for the day.

Perhaps you could do us a favour. The next time you're in the Valley of the Kings could you set up a direction sign. Nothing too elaborate, just something that says, "Kwik Bite, 2548 miles".

Best wishes,

Lindsay

To: Weight Watchers
From: James Spence
Subject: A Slim Chance

Hi there,

Just wanted to write to say how terrific Weight Watchers is. My first week trying out the 'Weight Watchers' scheme has just reached its climax. And what a whopper of a result! I've lost half a stone and feel 'inflated' by the prospects of future 'deflations'. See what I did there? It's called a play on words. But who am I to preach to you, the geniuses who invented thinness?

It was easy too! By counting up my points and balancing out my meals, I still got to eat some cake, drink a little wine, eat a few chocolate bars and even enjoy my favourite snack... jellied trotters with snouts in fish dribblings. Mmm. Makes the mouth water just thinking about it.

After being on the diet a week, a brilliant idea hit me, and I just had to write and share it with you. It is a suggestion to improve your diet, and I think it is one of those occasions where you'll kick yourselves for not thinking of it first: Why not lower the number of points on treats and raise the points on vegetables? That way, you'd eat just as much, but the food would be better.

I'm right aren't I? Let me know what you think. Anyway, I'll stick to your version for now as there may be some weird 'scientific' reason for keeping it your way (not that I believe in all that mumbo jumbo).

I also wondered if you could send me a Weight Watchers tee shirt so I could proudly display my new slim-line bod and endorse your company. XXL if you have one, if not, a XL or L will do nicely.

Many thanks and well done on a great diet! The mini muffins are too good to be true!!

Pass the carrots,

NO REPLY

James Spence

To: British Airways
From: James Spence
Subject: Come Fly With Me

Hi there,

I'm a long-term customer, and a huge fan of British Airways. I've flown many times and although I'm not a great flyer, I find your company strangely comforting. They always clean up any mess.

I write with a few ideas to help your business continue to expand:

- A hunk of cake: For every flight, a fistful of cake. My wife makes lovely cake, and she'd be willing to share recipes
- A cheaper service (but how? I hear you scream) You could have a much more 'risky' service without all this security nonsense or where you just attach a stamp and address sticker directly onto a passenger
- Surprise journeys to incorrect destinations. Everyone loves a surprise
- A helpful in-flight bear to snuggle on long journeys
- Perhaps a catchy beepy tune playing in the background while you fly. If the cheeky girls were serenading me as I flew, you can bet I'd come back for more
- If you bought your planes cheaper, you could pass that cheapness on to the consumer - Solution: competitor plane theft?
- A light person discount to motivate dieters
- A free tee shirt to anyone who sends in suggestions

I think you can see where this is going now: I would LOVE a British Airways tee shirt. If there was any way this could be arranged I'd be extremely happy.

Thanks for all you brilliant work. I love flying with BA.

Looking forward to many future flights,

James Spence

To:	CD WOW
From:	James Spence
Subject:	CD Story

G'Day CD WOW,

I have made many purchases with your fine organisation and I wanted to say a big thanks for all you do in keeping down the price of new music and DVDs. Time for an office group hug? I should say so. As a Doctor Who fan, I have made massive savings on your fine range of Doctor Who DVDs and other products.

I write because of an incident that occurred to me fairly recently. I often enjoy watching an episode of Doctor Who in the evening while my wife (Tiffany) performs a nightly stock-take of the fridge in case I've eaten more than my ration (I'm a hungry man). Normally this infuriates me, but not this particular evening when I found myself engrossed in the DVD "Doctor Who and the Caves of Androzani" bought from CD WOW. My viewing was somewhat interrupted when I saw that my cat (Angel: the beast from the east) had got locked in old man Jenkins' (my evil neighbour's) car.

To cut a long story short, I rescued the cat by constructing a crane-like device out of cornflake boxes, rope, twelve cans of grout, some lentils, a picture of Bill Odie and a bowler hat. I then was able to lower myself into the sunroof, thus allowing me to extract the silly feline. Sadly, I triggered an in-car defence system and a favourite tee shirt (it had a picture of an enraged monkey on it) was covered in sprout-juice. The tee shirt, my heroic chums, was destroyed but the cat was saved from sprout torture.

It then occurred to me! If I hadn't been enjoying Doctor Who in the first place, perhaps such a daring rescue may not have been necessary. I may have been paying closer attention to the cat and not the Timelord. And if your DVDs hadn't been so affordable on CD WOW, I may not have had the DVD in the first place. Now, I'm not the kind of puppy to lay blame at anyone's feet, but let's face it, sprout attack is not easily forgotten. I therefore wondered if you had a large CD WOW tee shirt for a loyal fan and customer to replace the one destroyed by enemy sprout-fire?

Thanks a million. Love the web site,

James Spence

To: Think! Road Safety Campaign
From: James Spence
Subject: Hedgehog Story

Dear Think!, the Road Safety Campaign,

As a busy woodland creature, I have little time to waste on foolish endeavours when I could be out rummaging up some grubs. However, I wanted to take a little time out to write and thank you for all your hard work in making the world a safer place for the likes of me and my pal Snouty Pete.

Your wondrous road safety campaign sends forth a delightful message more appealing than even a delicious buffet of slugs and snails. If it were not for your advice on crossing the road, I'd be a pancake right now, like poor old Uncle Prickle.

In order to help your campaign further, I have taken the liberty of drawing a poster for you to use in future road safety campaigns. Please see the attached image.

I wondered if you had any cool 'Think!' Road Safety stuff (tee shirts, pens, balloons, etc.) you could send me. I would like to share the message with Snouty Pete and (hopefully) save him from being bludgeoned into a two-dimensional flesh biscuit.

Keep up the great work,

James 'the Hedgehog' Spence

Department for Transport

Department for Transport
Great Minster House
76 Marsham Street
LONDON
SW1P 4DR

Tel: 020 7944 4097
Fax: 020 7944
Gtn: 3533

thank you for your email
Please find enclosed some freebies

Regards

A Hedgehog, 2 Tee Shirts, and Loads of Pens, Pencils and Erasers

THINK! Road Safety

BE SAFE BE SEEN
www.hedgehogs.gov.uk

To:	Olympic Games
From:	James Spence
Subject:	A Sporting Chance

Hi there Sports Fans,

I'm a huge fan of the Olympic Games, and am looking forward to it starting this afternoon. You can be assured that I'll be glued to the television throughout the entire games (sleep is for losers!)

At the last Olympics, I was so obsessed with watching the games I failed to notice when my horse was stolen by hoodlums right outside my caravan or when my favourite Olympics-watching tee shirt (it had a jolly dwarf on it) was destroyed by rats while hanging on the clothes line.

I know that when the Olympics first started, the athletes performed NUDE, but times have moved on and the invention of the tee shirt has made nudity redundant.

I wondered if you (or one of your many sponsors) had a tee shirt that you could send me? I'd be very grateful.

Thanks,

James 'the Olympian' Spence

To: Jewson
From: James Spence
Subject: Trojan Penguin

Dear Jewson,

I love visiting Jewson. I could spend hours wandering around investigating the different ways I could improve my home. I'll love Jewson until the day I DIY!

I write because of a strange event that happened to me recently. You may find this a little ...uncommon, but please read on my friends for every word of it is typed.

A few weeks back my house was attacked by penguins. That's right. Penguins. They had followed us home from the supermarket after witnessing us buying some fish. A long and arduous battle ensued (Battle Penguin) (involving the loss of several Knots Landing videos and my good friend and house guest Dr Sebastian becoming quite introverted).

Now, my friends, you may be wondering why I am even telling you this. The reason concerns the counter-strike that I, my wife (Tiffany), the cat (Angel) and my aforementioned good friend and house guest (Dr Sebastian Von Paws) made against the penguins to ensure no further attacks followed.

At first we tried attacking the South Pole directly, but those pesky penguins saw us coming, and hurled snow and eggs at us. It's one thing to defend your home from penguin attacks, but it is another to bring the fight to them. After several hours attempting to gain entry to their wintery world, we retreated to formulate a plan.

A quick visit to our local Jewson and we had all the components required to win this war. You see, I had assembled a giant 'wooden penguin' that we could hide in. We would leave it as a 'gift' for the emperor penguin. We covered it in marmalade to make it more appealing (penguins go nuts for marmalade - that's a fact the Zoo won't tell you about!). The plan went like clockwork and soon I had constructed the giant container.

We had concealed ourselves inside and the penguins fell for it! Bird brains! They took us through the gates of the South Pole. At midnight, once the penguins had gone to bed, we opened the door and sneaked out into the cold night, but alas! tragedy struck!

I am merely an intermediate DIY enthusiast, and had foolishly left a nail sticking out, which ripped my favourite tee shirt (it had a picture of a row of turnips on it) as I left the wooden structure. My cry awoke the penguins. Fortunately, I was able to calm the penguins down by telling them how I had built the giant penguin (penguins are DIY enthusiasts too!) The penguins were impressed with the quality of the materials and couldn't believe the low prices I quoted them.

As a result, a truce was found between penguins and humans and it was all thanks to Jewson.

You may be just about to pat yourselves on the back for allowing this truce to happen, but let's not race into that congratulatory back-slap just yet my friends. Let us not forget the loss of the tee shirt.

My wife suggested that perhaps I should contact the wonderful (God-like?) staff at Jewson. Yes, my friends, you could come to the rescue here too. Therefore I write to ask if you have any (large) Jewson tee shirts you could send to replace the one I lost to the penguins?

Thanks for everything Jewson. Especially thanks for saving the world from penguin attacks.

James 'The Penguin Slayer' Spence

TEE SHIRT

JEWSON

Jewson Limited
Customer Service Department
Merchant House
Binley Business Park
Coventry CV3 2TT
Tel: 0800 169 1616
Fax: 024 7656 0566
Website: www.jewson.co.uk

Our Ref: MY/32696

10/Jan/2005

Mr J Spence

Dear Mr J "Penguin Slayer" Spence,

Thank you for the details recently received in connection with the attack of penguins you have so unfortunately been the victim of.
Although we at Jewson do not advise actually attacking penguins in their home territory we are most pleased that you felt our merchandise up to the task of laying siege to them and commiserate most dearly with you over the loss of such a loyal t-shirt.
Of course hearing of your misfortune we dispatched a t-shirt immediately as a replacement, however the penguins not being the most efficient creatures in our temperate climate hired a crack band of mercenary attack squirrels who hi-jacked our delivery truck and made away with not only the t-shirt but also 3 bags of mixed nuts and a ham sandwich (no pickle). I'm sure that you are as grief stricken as ourselves to hear of this but there is now a ray of sunshine brightening the darkness as those kind people at Together (Cancer Research) have worked together with the Jewson T-shirt fairies to produce the item enclosed.
Hopefully this will help ease your pain and bring a small glimmer of light to your day.

Yours sincerely,

Marc Yates
Customer Ser

To:	Weetabix
From:	James Spence
Subject:	Badgerbix

Dear Weetabix

My wife and I believe there is a badger living at the bottom of the garden! Furthermore, the stripy little fellow loves Weetabix!

It all began two weeks ago. My wife was upstairs getting changed when, out of the corner of her eye, she caught a glimpse of something in the bushes outside. Her curiosity aroused, she went out to investigate but found nothing there except flattened plants suggesting that something had been sitting in the undergrowth.

She thought no more about it. However, the next day, as she was drying off after a bath, she became aware of a flashing light coming from the same bush. Again she investigated and this time found an empty box of Weetabix!

Upon further investigation, we discovered a large hole in the fence behind the bush. There was only one explanation. A badger must have found the box of Weetabix and created a way into our garden so that he could sit in the bushes eating the delicious wheat goodness.

My wife has become so excited about seeing the badger that she now always keeps the window open while she showers so that she can keep an eye out for it. From time to time she sees a flash from the bushes, which we assume must be the glint in the badger's eye.

We now leave out boxes of Weetabix for him, and he always empties them. He's mad for Weetabix!

But wait! The story developed last night as I desposited another box of Weetabix. We found a camera case! It looks like a nature photographer must have found the badger's hiding place and squeezed in to take photographs of the badger enjoying his breakfast. I wouldn't be surprised if the black and white rascal appeared in a nature magazine eating his tasty wheat treats!

I wondered if you happened to have a Large Weetabix tee shirt which my wife could wear when she looks for the badger, as we think it would endear her to him, and he'd be less likely to run away and hide.

Sincerely,

James Spence

Reference: **425466**-ns/jed
Enclosure:
1 x Weetabix T-Shirt

05/08/2008

Mr James Spence

Dear Mr Spence

Many thanks for your email.

Over the years we have heard from many animal lovers telling us of their furry and feathered friend's fondness for our products. From kittens and puppies to rescued ducks and hedgehogs, we have probably covered most of the animal kingdom (though I cannot recall a badger story before!) It all goes to show how versatile our 'breakfast' cereals really are.

We are delighted to hear your badger enjoys Weetabix so much and trust he will continue to do so for a long time to come.

Once again, thank you for taking the time to contact us. It was great to hear from you. We do hope you will accept the enclosed, sent with our compliments.

Yours sincerely

Dan Herrin
Consumer Services Manager
01536 721566

To: Abercrombie & Fitch
From: James Spence
Subject: Jeremy

Greeting Clothes Makers,

Isn't it a fine day for a walk, I said to myself this very morning. I admit there was a chill in the air and the threat of rain overhead, but on the whole it seemed like a most pleasant morning for a brisk stroll. You see, my good friends and potential flat-mates, the cold air posed no threat to me, for I am the proud owner of a rather fetching Abercrombie and Fitch sweater. It is a fine sweater and I have named it Jeremy. Jeremy and I have done the following things together:

- had a bath
- limbo danced through a forest
- huddled beside to a bonfire for warmth
- contemplated world events whilst holding aloft a cucumber
- hunted a paper tiger with a staple gun
- sky-diving (from the top of a bus as we did not have access to a plane)
- miscellaneous things with fish
- handbag shopping
- invaded Belgium in a canoe
- looked smashing
- made copious quantities of tea
- picked up the cat (Angel)
- picked cat hair off my beloved sweater (not such an Angel it seems)
- various other tasks

I love my Jeremy, but he craves company. Can you send me him a large tee shirt?

Hooray for Jeremy,

James Spence

NO REPLY

To:	Kwik Fit
From:	James Spence
Subject:	Fit As a Fiddle

Good Day Kwik Fit Fitters,

The last time I visited Kwik Fit I had a most unusual experience and I wanted to tell you about it as it changed my perception of Kwik Fit staff forever.

After a particularly challenging stunt had gone awry, I took my car to Kwik Fit to replace the tyre that had melted. As is the norm with my visits to Kwik Fit, I had brought a book to read whilst the professional engineers and mechanics set to work on reinstating the roadworthiness of my vehicle.

As I turned the pages of my Biggles adventure, I enjoyed the heat of the office and the hot chocolate I had made myself. Occasionally, my head slumped forward. I soon was no longer aware of what was going on around me.

All that changed, moments later, when I became aware of a swishing, soaring sound. I replaced my bookmark and turned my head to investigate the source of this noise. Good people, what I saw took me wholly by surprise. One of your Kwik Fit fitters was flying around the garage, in the style of a comic book super hero!!! Outrageous!

Now, I'm not against the use of super powers in the right place, such as saving babies from house fires, the timely untying of damsels from railway lines or rotating the world backwards on its axis to turn back time in order to rescue your 'bit of skirt'. However, this particular use of unaided flight was surely a Health and Safety hazard. I watched the display, transfixed, until I felt myself being shaken by a member of your staff.

I felt strangely groggy, and noticed that in all the excitement of the flying man, someone (perhaps a member of your staff?) had drooled down the front of my tee shirt, ruining it completely!

When my car was finally returned to me, the work carried out was first class. In fact, it was better than new! However, the incident of the flying staff member and the hot chocolately drool has tarnished an otherwise first rate service.

I write to you now, to enquire as to whether you had a Kwik Fit tee shirt that you could send me to replace the one that was lost on that fateful day. If the answer is yes, I'll be cock-a-hoop!! If the answer is no, I'll get over it, but not without counselling of some variety.

Anyway, thanks for all the hard work you've put into fixing my car over the years and well done on employing such friendly staff.

Up, up and away,

James Spence

"Ode to Mr Spence"

Dear Mr Spence … here is our reply
To the e-mail that you kindly sent
We were impressed by your grammatical expertise
That is a sentiment sincerely meant

We know our fitters are really good
And mostly they are breathtakingly fast
However, we're puzzled about a fitter "flying"
And with more info ..he'll be pinned straight to the mast

In closing, thank you for your letter
And we note the points that made you write
Please find enclosed a "chocolate free" Kwik-Fit top
And we trust that the matter is now right,

To:	Mum & Dad
From:	James
Subject:	Hey Folks!

Dear Mum and Dad,

First off, I'd like to say an enormous thanks for giving me life, protecting me from harm, providing a wonderful home to grow up in, for supporting my education, making sure I had a happy childhood, for chauffeuring me around, then later for my many, many driving lessons, for paying me into movies, for the general support you've given me in life, all my pocket money, for making me brush my teeth, for the awesome toys I had as a kid, for my wedding, for your unconditional love, for my good looks, my modesty, your sensible advice, for all the car maintenance, for the stuffed bear named Dr Sebastian, for your generosity and a heck of a lot of cups of tea. There's probably other stuff as well, but I don't want to labour the point.

Anyway, thanks.

The bad news, Mum and Dad, is that my demands on your income are not over. As your (favourite?) child, I feel that I am entitled to a free tee shirt (perhaps bearing some sort of family logo?), and maybe some vouchers for free food (the good stuff, not one of Dad's mystery ingredient fry ups).

Unfortunately I cannot promise that this will be the last time you fork out your hard-earned cash on me, as you know I am very fond of freebies and you live so close.

I look forward to your written reply enclosing the items discussed above, or cash equivalent.

Yours Sincerely,

James (Your Son)

To: James
From: Mum & Dad
Subject: Re: Hey Folks!

Hi Jimbo,

We only did it for the Family Allowance payments!

Love,

Dad